THE CAT WHO CAME IN
OFF THE ROOF

The CAT WHO CAME IN off the ROOF

ANNIE M. G. SCHMIDT

Translated from the Dutch by David Colmer

A Yearling Book

English translation copyright © 2014 by David Colmer
Cover art and interior illustrations copyright © 2016 by Eda Kaban

All rights reserved. Published in the United States by Yearling, an imprint of Random House Children's Books, a division of Penguin Random House LLC, New York. Originally published in hardcover in Dutch as *Minoes* in Amsterdam, The Netherlands, in 1970. *Minoes* copyright © 1970 by the Estate of Annie M. G. Schmidt. Subsequently published in hardcover in the United States by Delacorte Press, an imprint of Random House Children's Books, New York, in 2016.

This English translation was first published in paperback by Pushkin Children's Books, London, in 2014.

Yearling and the jumping horse design are registered trademarks of Penguin Random House LLC.

Visit us on the Web! randomhousekids.com

Educators and librarians, for a variety of teaching tools, visit us at RHTeachersLibrarians.com

The Library of Congress has cataloged the hardcover edition of this work as follows:
Schmidt, Annie M. G.
[Minoes. English]
The cat who came in off the roof / Annie M. G. Schmidt ; translated from the Dutch by David Colmer.
pages cm
Originally published in Amsterdam by De Arbeiderspers in 1970 under title: Minoes.
Summary: Minou, formerly a cat but now a woman with many cattish ways, helps Tibble, a newspaper reporter, with information she gets from her many feline friends.
ISBN 978-0-553-53500-6 (trade hc) — ISBN 978-0-553-53503-7 (library binding)
ISBN 978-0-553-53501-3 (ebook) [1. Cats—Fiction. 2. Reporters and reporting—Fiction. 3. Shapeshifting—Fiction.] I. Colmer, David, translator.
II. Title.
PZ7.S3497Cat 2016
[Fic]—dc23
2015008470

ISBN 978-0-553-53502-0 (pbk.)

Printed in the United States of America
10 9 8 7 6 5 4 3 2 1
First Yearling Edition 2017

CONTENTS

CONTENTS

— 1 —

NO NEWS ANYWHERE

"Tibble! Where's Tibble? Has anyone seen Tibble? The boss wants to talk to him. Where's he got to? *Tibble!*"

Tibble had heard them, all right. But he'd slipped down out of sight. And now he was crouched behind his desk trembling and thinking, I don't want to talk to the boss, I'm too scared. I know exactly what's going to happen. He's going to fire me.

"Ah, Tibble! There you are!"

Oh, no. They'd spotted him.

"The boss wants to see you straightaway."

He couldn't get out of it now. He had no choice but to walk down the corridor with his head hanging and stop at the door marked *Editor*.

He knocked. A voice said, "Yes."

When Tibble went in, his boss was on the phone. He pointed at an empty chair and carried on with his conversation.

Tibble sat down and waited.

This was in the building of the *Killenthorn Courier*, the newspaper Tibble worked for. Writing articles.

"So, Tibble," the editor said as he hung up the phone. "There's something important we need to discuss."

Here it comes, thought Tibble.

"These articles you write . . . They're quite good. Sometimes, even *very* good."

Tibble smiled. Maybe it wasn't going to be too bad, after all.

"But . . ."

Tibble waited patiently. Of course, there had to be a "but." Otherwise he wouldn't be sitting here.

"But . . . there's never any *news* in them. I've told you so many times. Your articles are always about cats."

Tibble was quiet for a moment. It was true. He was a real cat lover. He knew all the local cats. He even had one himself.

"But yesterday I wrote an article that didn't even mention cats," he said. "It was about spring."

"Exactly," his boss said. "It was about spring. About the little leaves appearing on the trees. Is that *news*?"

"Er . . . they were *new* leaves," Tibble said.

His boss sighed. "Listen carefully, Tibble," he said. "I like you. You're a nice guy, and you can string a story together. But we're working on a *news*paper here. And a *news*paper has to provide *news*. It has to tell people things they don't know."

"But it's already full of news," Tibble said. "Wars and stuff like that. And murders. I thought people would like to read about cats and leaves for a change."

2

"I'm afraid not, Tibble. Don't get me wrong, you don't need to write about murders or bank robberies. But a small town like ours is full of little news stories. You just have to find them. I've told you again and again, you're too shy. You have to approach people. You have to ask questions. But you're always too scared. Apparently you only ever associate with cats."

Again Tibble remained silent, because it was true. He *was* shy. And if you work for a newspaper, you can't afford to be shy. If you want to find out about things other people don't know about, you have to march right up to strangers. You have to be brave enough to barge in on a government minister, even if he's having a bath. And then you have to ask fearlessly, "Where were you last night?"

A good newspaperman does things like that. But not Tibble.

"Well," the editor said, "I'll give you one last chance. From now on, write articles with news in them. I want the first one on my desk tomorrow morning. And after that, I want to see two or three a week. And if you can't manage it . . ."

Tibble understood perfectly. If he didn't come up with something, he'd lose his job.

"Goodbye, Tibble."

"Goodbye, sir."

And now he was walking down the street. Light rain was falling, and everything looked gray. Tibble was taking his time. He was looking around and keeping his eyes peeled and his ears open. But there was no news anywhere. He couldn't see anything new. There was nothing he didn't already know about.

He saw cars. Parked cars and cars driving down the street. There were a few pedestrians and the occasional cat. But he wasn't allowed to write about cats anymore. In the end he was so tired he sat down on a bench in Green Square, under a tree where it was still dry.

There was already somebody else sitting on the bench, and now Tibble saw who it was. It was his old teacher from school, Mr. Smith.

"Look who we have here," said Mr. Smith. "What a nice surprise, bumping into you like this. I've heard you've got a job with the *Courier*. I was always sure you'd end up at a newspaper. It's going fabulously, I suppose."

Tibble swallowed uncomfortably and said, "I'm settling in."

"You always wrote such wonderful compositions at school," Mr. Smith said. "I knew you'd go far. Yes, you're an excellent writer."

"Can't *you* tell me something I don't know?" Tibble asked.

Mr. Smith was quite insulted. "Has it gone to your head already?" he asked. "I tell you how well you write and you ask me to tell you something you don't know. . . . That's not very nice of you."

"Oh, I didn't mean it like that!" Tibble cried, blushing. He was about to explain what he *had* meant, but before he got a chance there was the sound of furious barking close by. They both looked up. A big German shepherd was racing after something, but they couldn't quite make out what that something was. It disappeared between two parked cars and the dog rushed after it. The very next instant there was a wild rustling in the tall elm tree near the cars.

"A cat," Mr. Smith said. "A cat's been treed."

"Was it a cat?" Tibble asked. "It was big. And it kind of fluttered a little. It looked more like a large bird. A stork or something like that."

"Storks don't run," Mr. Smith said.

"No, but it definitely fluttered. And cats don't flutter."

They went over to have a look.

The dog was standing under the tree and still barking furiously.

They tried to see what exactly was up there between all those branches, but the cat was completely hidden. If it *was* a cat.

"Mars! Here, boy!" Someone was calling the dog. "*Mars*, here!"

A man appeared with a leash. He clicked the leash onto the dog's collar and started pulling.

"*Grrr* . . . ," said Mars, holding his four legs stiff as the man dragged him away over the road. Tibble and Mr. Smith kept peering up for a moment. And now they saw something very high up among the new leaves.

A leg. A leg in a stylish stocking with a shiny, high-heeled shoe on the foot.

"Heavens," said Mr. Smith. "It's a lady."

"It can't be," Tibble said. "That high up? How'd she get up there so quickly?"

Now a face appeared too. A frightened face with big scared eyes and masses of red hair.

"Is it gone?" she called.

"It's gone! Come on down!" Tibble called back.

"I'm too scared," she moaned. "It's so far."

Tibble looked around. There was a van parked close by.

Cautiously, he climbed onto the roof of the van and reached out as far as he could with one hand. The woman crawled slowly to the end of her branch, then lowered herself onto another and grabbed Tibble's hand.

She turned out to be tremendously agile. In one easy leap

she was on the roof of the van, and a second hop took her down to the street.

"I dropped my case," she said. "Have you seen it anywhere round here?"

It was lying in the gutter. Mr. Smith picked it up for her.

"Here," he said. "Your clothes are all messed up too."

She brushed the dirt and leaves off her skirt and jacket and said, "It was such a big dog. . . . I can't help it, I just *have* to get up into a tree when I see a dog coming. Thanks very much for your help."

Tibble suddenly remembered his article and realized he should stop her to ask a few questions. This was definitely something unusual he could write about.

But he hesitated a little too long. He was too shy again. And off she went with that small case of hers.

"What a peculiar young woman," Mr. Smith said. "She was like a cat."

"Yes," said Tibble. "She was just like a cat."

They watched her walk off. She went round a corner.

I can still catch up with her, thought Tibble. He left Mr. Smith behind without saying goodbye and raced down the narrow street he'd seen her take. There she was. He'd ask her, "Excuse me, but I was wondering if you could tell me why you're so scared of dogs and how you're able to climb trees so fast. . . ."

But suddenly he couldn't see her anymore.

Had she gone into one of the houses? But in this part of the street there weren't any doors. Only a long stretch of fence with a garden on the other side. There wasn't a gate in the fence either; she must have slipped through the bars. Tibble peered through the fence at the garden. He could see a lawn and quite a few shrubs. But no young lady.

"She must have gone in through a door somewhere," Tibble said. "I must have just missed it. And the rain's getting heavier. I'm going home."

On the way he bought two fish and a bag of pears for his dinner. Tibble lived in an attic. It was a very nice attic with one big room he used as a living room *and* a bedroom. Plus a small kitchen, a tiny bathroom and a junk room. He had to climb a lot of stairs, but once he was up there he had a view out over lots of roofs and chimneys. His big gray cat, Fluff, was sitting there waiting for him.

"You can smell the fish, can't you?" Tibble said. "Come into the kitchen and then we'll cook them and eat them. You're getting a whole fish tonight, Fluff. And it might be the last time I can afford to buy fish at all, because tomorrow I'm going to get fired. Tomorrow I get the boot, Fluff. And then I won't earn a penny. We'll have to go out begging."

"*Mrow*," said Fluff.

"Unless I manage to write a news article tonight," Tibble said. "But it's already too late for that."

He sliced some bread and made some tea, then ate in the kitchen with Fluff. And then he went into the living room and sat down at his typewriter.

Maybe I can write something about that strange lady after all. And he started.

This afternoon, at approximately five p.m., a German shepherd chased a lady across Green Square. She was terrified and shot up one of the tall elms, all the way to the top. As she was too scared to climb down again, I lent a helping hand. She then resumed her walk before slipping through the bars of a fence and into a garden.

Tibble read through it. It was a very *short* article. And he felt like his boss would only say, "It's about a cat *again*."

He had to do better. First a peppermint, he thought. That will clear my head.

He searched his desk for the roll of peppermints.

Huh, I was sure I had a roll of peppermints somewhere. "Do you know where I put the peppermints, Fluff?"

"*Mrow*," said Fluff.

"I didn't think so. What's the matter, do you want to go out again? Are you so keen to get back out on the roof?"

Tibble opened the kitchen window and Fluff disappeared into the darkness out on the roof.

It was still drizzling, and a gust of cold wind blew in.

Tibble went back to his typewriter, put in a clean sheet of paper, and started over again.

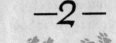

—2—
A STRAY CAT

While Tibble was fretting and worrying in his attic, the strange young lady was closer than he thought.

Just a couple of streets away she was sitting in a garden, tucked in behind some shrubs. Night had fallen, and it was pitch-black. A strong wind was blowing, and the garden was extremely wet.

She sat there with her little case and made a small mewing noise. First nothing happened.

She made the noise again. And now an answer came from the direction of the house.

"*Mew . . .*"

An ancient but very dignified black cat came walking toward her very slowly, then stopped suspiciously, some distance from the shrubs.

"Aunt Sooty . . . ," the young lady whispered.

The old cat spat and shrunk back.

"Now I see . . . ," she hissed. "*You!*"

"Do you still recognize me, Aunt Sooty?"

"You're Minou! My niece Minou from Victoria Avenue!"

"That's right. I heard you were living here, and here I am."

"I've already heard about it," the old cat said nervously. "About what happened to you . . . all the cats are talking about it. How could something like that happen, Minou? To you, a member of one of Killenthorn's very best cat families! What does your sister say?"

"She doesn't want to know me anymore," the young lady said. "She says it must be my own fault. She gave me the cold tail. . . ."

"*Ssss* . . . ," said Aunt Sooty. "I can't blame her. You must have done something ghastly to be punished like this. Turned into a *human*! What a horrific punishment. I wouldn't be human for all the canaries in China. Tell me, was it a magic spell?"

"I don't know," Minou said.

"But you must know *how* it happened."

"I went out as a cat and came back as a human, that's all I know."

"Incredible," Aunt Sooty said. "But it must have been your fault. You probably did something terribly *uncattish*. What was it?"

"Nothing. I didn't do anything. Not as far as I know."

"And you're wearing clothes," Aunt Sooty continued. "Did you have them on straightaway?"

"I . . . I found them somewhere," Minou said. "I couldn't roam the streets naked."

"Ugh! And you have a *case* . . . ," Aunt Sooty hissed. "What's the point of that?"

"I found it too."

"What's in it?"

"Pajamas. And a toothbrush. And a washcloth and some soap."

"So you don't wash yourself with spit anymore?"

"No."

"Then all is lost," Aunt Sooty said. "I'd still hoped that it might come good. But now I'm afraid there's no hope for you at all."

"Aunt Sooty, I'm hungry. Do you have anything I can eat?"

"I'm sorry, not a thing. I've already finished this evening's Kit-e-kat. And I have a very tidy human. She never leaves food lying around. Everything always goes straight back in the fridge."

"Is she nice?" Minou asked.

"Absolutely. Why?"

"Maybe she'd like to have me too?"

"No!" Aunt Sooty cried, horrified. "Child, the thought of it. The way you are now?"

"I'm looking for a home, Aunt Sooty. I need somewhere to stay. Can't you think of anywhere? Here in the neighborhood?"

"I'm old," Aunt Sooty said. "I almost never make it up onto the rooftops anymore. I hardly even go into other cats' gardens. But I still have a few acquaintances left. One garden up, there's Mr. Smith's cat, the teacher's. That way. Go and talk to him. He's called Simon. Cross-Eyed Simon. He's Siamese, but perfectly friendly."

"And you think maybe that teacher would . . ."

"No!" Aunt Sooty said. "You can't stay there either. But Simon knows all the cats in the whole neighborhood. And that means he knows all the humans too. He can probably point you in the right direction."

"Thank you, Aunt Sooty. Bye. I'll drop by again soon."

"If it doesn't work out, talk to the Tatter Cat. A stray. You can usually find her on the roof of the Social Security Building. Not that she has a particularly good reputation, of course. She's a scruff and a tramp. But very well informed, because of all the time she spends on the streets."

"Thanks."

"And now I'm going inside," Aunt Sooty said. "I am deeply sorry for you, Minou, but I still think you must have done something to deserve it. And one last piece of advice: Wash yourself with spit. Lick yourself. That is the beginning and end of all wisdom."

With her tail held high, Aunt Sooty strolled off through the garden and back to the house while her poor niece picked up her case and crawled through a hole in the hedge. Off in search of the cat next door.

Tibble wasn't doing well. He paced the floor of his attic and sat down every now and then at his typewriter, only to tear up everything he'd typed in a rage and rummage through the drawers in search of his peppermints. He had the idiotic idea that he couldn't think or write without a peppermint, but meanwhile it was getting later and later.

"I should actually go back out," he said. "To see if anything's happening anywhere. Something I can write about. But I don't think anyone's out on the street anymore with this weather. Strange that Fluff's staying out on the roof so long. Usually he comes back a lot sooner. I think I'll just go to bed. Tomorrow I'll go up to the boss and say, 'I'm sorry, you're right. I don't have what it takes to be a newspaperman.' And he'll say, 'Yes, I think it would be best if you started looking for something else.' And that will be that. I'll go and look for another job."

There was a quiet noise in the kitchen.

It was the bin.

"That's Fluff," Tibble said. "The scrounger! He's trying to get the fish bones out of the bin. Even though he's already had a whole fish. I'd better go have a look, otherwise he'll tip the whole bin over and I'll have to clean it all up."

Tibble got up and opened the door to the kitchen.

He was shocked by what he saw.

It wasn't Fluff. It was a woman. The young lady from the tree, who was now digging around in his rubbish bin. There was only one way she could have gotten in—through the window that opened out onto the roof.

The moment she heard him, she spun around just as she was stuffing a big fish skeleton into her mouth with her paws. No, no . . . with her *hands*, Tibble thought immediately, but she looked so much like a wet, timid stray cat that he'd almost gone, "Psssst, scat!" But he didn't say a word.

She took the bones back out of her mouth and gave him a friendly smile. Her green eyes were slightly slanted.

"I'm sorry," she said. "I was just sitting on the roof with your cat, Fluff. And it smelt so delicious. That's why I stepped in through the window for a moment. He's still out there."

She had a very respectable and ladylike way of talking. But

she was soaked through. Her red hair was stuck to her head in clumps, and her jacket and skirt were sopping and formless.

And suddenly he felt so sorry for her. She was just like a sad, half-drowned cat. A hungry stray!

"I'm afraid we ate all the fish," Tibble said. "But if you like . . . I could give you a sauc—" He'd almost said a saucer of milk. ". . . a glass of milk. And a sandwich, perhaps? With sardines?"

"Yes, please," she said politely, but meanwhile she was dizzy and wild-eyed with hunger.

"Perhaps you can put that back, then," Tibble said, pointing at the skeleton in her hand.

She dropped it in the bin. And there she sat, shy and wet on a kitchen chair, watching Tibble open a tin of sardines.

"May I ask your name?" Tibble said.

"Minou. *Miss* Minou."

"I'm—"

"Mr. Tibble," she said. "I know."

"Just Tibble. Everyone calls me Tibble."

"If you don't mind, I'd rather stick to *Mr.* Tibble."

"What were you doing up on the roof?" he asked.

"I, um . . . I was looking for a job."

Tibble looked at her with surprise. "On the roof?"

But she didn't answer. The sandwiches were ready. Tibble went to put the plate down on the floor, but changed his mind. She probably eats like a person, he thought. And he was right. She ate her sandwiches very daintily, with little bites and nibbles.

"You have a job at the newspaper," she said between mouthfuls. "But not for long."

"How do you know that?" Tibble cried.

"It's what I heard," she said. "That article didn't work out. The one about me up the tree. Too bad."

"Now, stop right there," Tibble said. "I'd like very much to know who told you that. I haven't spoken to anyone about that at all."

He waited until her mouth was empty. It was the last bite. She picked up the last crumbs with a finger and licked it clean.

Then she half closed her eyes.

She's falling asleep, Tibble thought.

But she didn't go to sleep. She sat there staring sweetly into space. And now Tibble heard a soft rumbling noise. Minou was purring.

"I asked you something," Tibble said.

"Oh, yes," she said. "Well . . . it's just something I heard."

Tibble sighed. Then he noticed that she was shivering. No wonder, with all those wet clothes.

"Don't you have anything dry to put on?"

"Yes," she said. "In my case."

Only now did Tibble notice that she still had her case with her. It was on the floor under the window.

"You should have a hot shower," he said. "And change into something dry. Otherwise you'll catch your death. The bathroom's just there."

"Thanks very much," she said. She stepped across the room to pick up her case, and when she passed him on the way back she pushed her head up against his arm for a moment, wriggling her shoulders slightly at the same time.

Tibble jumped back as if a crocodile was trying to bite him. She's rubbing up against me! he thought.

Once she'd closed the bathroom door behind her, Tibble sat down in the living room. "This is mad," he said to himself. "A strange woman comes in through the attic window. Half starved. Then purrs and rubs up against you!"

Suddenly something terrible occurred to him. Surely she doesn't . . . she won't want to stay with me, will she? She was looking for a job, she'd said. But she was obviously looking for somewhere to live. Like a cat looking for a new home.

"I don't want her here," Tibble said. "I've already got a cat. I'm way too happy living alone and doing my own thing. And anyway, I've only got one bed. I should never have let her use the shower!"

Here she was again . . . coming back into the room.

See! Tibble said to himself. Just as I thought. She was standing there in her pajamas with a dressing gown on over the top and slippers on her feet.

She gestured at the wet two-piece suit she was holding draped over one arm. "Is it all right if I dry this in front of the fire?"

"Um . . . yes, go ahead," Tibble said. "But I want to say straight away that you, um . . ."

"What?"

"Look, Miss Minou, it's fine for you to sit down for an hour or so until your clothes dry. But you can't stay here."

"No?"

"No. I'm sorry. That's absolutely out of the question."

"Oh," she said. "Not even for just one night?"

"No," Tibble said. "I don't have a bed for you."

"I don't need a bed. Back there in the junk room there's a big box. A cardboard box that used to have tinned soup in it."

"A box?" Tibble said. "You want to sleep in a box?"

"Absolutely. If you put some fresh newspaper in it first."

Tibble shook his head stubbornly. "I'll give you some money for a hotel," he said. "There's one just around the corner."

He reached for his wallet, but she refused point-blank. "Oh, no," she said. "There's no need. If it's really not possible, I'll just be off. I'll put my wet clothes back on and leave at once."

She stood there looking pitiful. And with such a frightened look on her face. And outside you could hear the wind and the rain. You couldn't possibly send a poor cat out onto the roof in weather like this.

"All right, fine, but just one night," Tibble said.

"Can I sleep in the box?"

"If you like. But under one condition. You have to tell me how you knew all those things about me. Who I am and where I work and what kind of article I was trying to write."

They heard a small flopping sound in the kitchen. It was Fluff, finally back from his roof walk and coming in with wet gray fur.

"He told me," Minou said, pointing at Fluff. "He told me all about you. And actually, I've spoken to lots of cats who live around here. They all said you were the nicest."

Tibble blushed. He felt strangely flattered. "You . . . you talk to cats?" he asked.

"Yes."

What nonsense, thought Tibble. The woman's quite mad.

"And, er . . . how did you come to be able to talk to cats?"

"I was one myself," she said.

Totally bonkers, thought Tibble.

Minou had sat down in front of the fire, next to Fluff. They

17

were sitting together on the rug, and Tibble could now hear two purring sounds mixed together. It sounded very peaceful. Shall I write that article about her after all? Tibble thought.

> *Last night I provided shelter to a purring lady who entered my apartment through the attic window and, on being asked, informed me that she had once been a cat. . . .*

I'd be out on my ear the same day, thought Tibble. Now he could hear them talking to each other, the young lady and the cat. They were making little purring, meowy kinds of noises.

"What's Fluff saying now?" he asked as a joke.

"He says your peppermints are in a jam jar on the top shelf of the bookcase. You put them there yourself."

Tibble stood up to have a look. She was right.

—3—
THE TATTER CAT

"I still don't believe it," Tibble said. "You being able to talk to cats. It must be something else. Some kind of mind-reading or something."

"Maybe," Minou said dreamily. She yawned. "It's time for me to get in my box. Can I take this old paper?"

"Are you sure you don't need a blanket or a pillow or anything?"

"No, no, not at all. Fluff likes to sleep on your feet, so I've heard. Everyone has their own preference. Good night."

"Good night, Miss Minou."

At the door she turned round for a moment. "I heard a bit of news while I was out and about," she said. "On the roofs here in the neighborhood."

"News? What kind of news?"

"The Tatter Cat is due to have another litter any time now."

"Oh," said Tibble. "It's a shame, but I'm not allowed to write about cats anymore. They say it's not interesting enough."

"Too bad," said Minou.

"Did you hear anything else?"

"Just about Mr. Smith being so sad."

"Mr. Smith? Do you mean the schoolteacher? I was talking to him today. He's the one who helped me get you down out of the tree. He didn't look sad."

"He is, though."

"That doesn't sound like interesting news either," Tibble said. "Is he just down in the dumps or is it something in particular?"

"Next week it will be twenty-five years since he was made head teacher at the school," Minou said. "He was really hoping there'd be some kind of festivities. An anniversary celebration. But, no."

"Why not?"

"Nobody knows about it. Everyone's forgotten. He thought people would remember . . . but they haven't."

"Can't he remind them?"

"He refuses. He's too proud. That's what Cross-Eyed Simon says."

"Cross-Eyed Simon? That's his Siamese."

"Exactly. He's the one I spoke to. And he told me all about it. And now I'm going to get into my box."

She said a quick "*Mrow*" to Fluff. And Fluff said "*Mreeow*" in reply. That was probably "Sleep tight."

Tibble grabbed the phone book. It was much too late at night, but he still dialed Mr. Smith's number.

"I'm sorry for calling so late," Tibble blurted, "but I just heard that you'll be celebrating an anniversary soon. Twenty-five years as head teacher. Is that right?"

There was a long silence on the other end of the line. Then Mr. Smith said, "So some people have remembered."

"No, cats . . ." Tibble was about to say, but he stopped himself just in time.

"Of course they have," he said instead. "How could anyone forget something like that? You don't mind me writing an article about it, do you?"

"I'd be delighted," said Mr. Smith.

"Could I drop by to talk to you about it? It is *rather* late . . . but I would very much like to hand in the article tomorrow morning. Something about your life and about the school . . ."

"Come straight over," said Mr. Smith.

It was three in the morning by the time Tibble got back home again. He had a pad full of notes about Mr. Smith's life and work. He tiptoed through the attic and, before sitting down at the typewriter, peeked into the junk room.

Minou was curled up in the box asleep.

She saved me, thought Tibble. I've got an article. I just have to write it up.

When he finally went to bed, he told a sleepy Fluff: "I'll hand it in tomorrow. It's a good article. And it's real news."

Fluff lay down on his feet and went back to sleep.

I'll thank her in the morning . . . this strange Miss Minou, Tibble thought, and then he fell asleep too.

But when he got up the next morning she was gone.

The box was empty. There was fresh newspaper spread out over the bottom, and everything had been left neat and tidy. Her clothes were gone as well and so was her case.

"Did she say anything, Fluff, before she left?"

"*Mrow* . . . ," said Fluff. But Tibble didn't understand.

"Well," he said. "I'm actually quite relieved. I've got my attic to myself again."

Then he saw the article lying on his desk. "It's fantastic," he cried out loud. "I'm going into the office and I've got something for the paper. They won't fire me. At least . . . not today." His happiness disappeared. He'd be trudging around town again tonight searching for another story.

There was a smell of coffee. He went into the kitchen and saw that Miss Minou had made some coffee for him. And done the dishes too. That was nice.

The window was open. She'd left the way she'd come: through the attic window.

At least the weather's better, Tibble thought. She won't have to wander around in the rain. He wondered if she was out talking to cats again? If she'd stayed here . . . he thought. If I'd let her stay . . . maybe she'd have brought some news home for me every day. He felt like shouting out through the window, over the rooftops, "Puss, puss, puss . . . Mi-nou!"

But he restrained himself. "Bah, how selfish can you get?" he said to himself. "You only want to let her stay because you think there might be something in it for you. What a nasty character trait! Forget about her and find your own news. Don't be so shy. Anyway, she's gone for good. She's probably miles away by now."

But at that moment Minou was very close by. She was sitting on the roof of the Social Security Building, the highest roof in the vicinity. She was talking to the Tatter Cat.

The Tatter Cat was called that because she was battered and tattered. She was always dirty, and she usually had muddy paws. Her tail was thin and wispy, there was a chunk out of her left ear, and her coat was drab and patchy.

"Your kittens are due soon," Minou said.

"Oh, put a cork in it," said the Tatter Cat. "Sometimes I wonder if it's ever going to stop. My whole life's one stinking litter after the other."

"How many children do you have?" Minou asked.

The Tatter Cat scratched herself at length. "How would I bleedin' know?" she said. She had a filthy mouth. But living on the street will do that to a cat. "Anyway, let's not talk about me," the Tatter Cat said. "This thing with you is much, much worse. How can something like that even exist? What did it?"

She stared at Minou with fear in her yellow eyes.

"I wish I knew. And the worst thing is, I'm not even *all* human. It's all so half and half."

"But you are all human. From head to toe."

"I mean *inside*," Minou said. "I still have almost all my cattish characteristics. I purr, I hiss, I rub up against people. I wash with a washcloth, but otherwise . . . I wonder if I still like mice. I'll have to try one."

"Do you still know the Great Yawl-Yowl Song?" the Tatter Cat asked.

"I think so."

"Sing a few bars, then."

Minou opened her mouth and a horrific, raucous caterwauling came out of it, a howling, shrieking, wailing sound.

The Tatter Cat joined in immediately, and together they screeched at the top of their voices. They kept going until someone opened a nearby attic window and hurled a large empty bottle at them. It hit the roof between them and smashed to pieces, driving them apart.

"All in the game!" the Tatter Cat cried cheerfully. "You know what? It's only temporary! You'll get over it. Someone who sings as well as you do *stays* cat. Feel your upper lip. You sure you don't have any whiskers?"

Minou felt her lip. "No," she said.

"And your tail? How's that?"

"Gone completely."

"Do you feel sometimes to see if it's growing back?"

"Of course. But there's no sign of it. Not even a tiny little bump."

"Have you got a house?" the Tatter Cat asked.

"I thought I did for a while . . . but I think it's off."

"With the young guy from the paper?"

"Yes," said Minou. "I'm still kind of hoping he'll call me. I left my case over there behind a chimney, in the gutter."

"You're much better off on the streets," the Tatter Cat said. "The life of a stray. Come with me. I'll introduce you to tons of my kids. Most of 'em have really made something of themselves. One of my sons is the cafeteria cat in the factory. And one of my daughters is the Council Cat. She lives in the town hall. And then there's—"

"Shhh . . . be quiet for a sec," Minou said.

They stopped talking. From across the roofs they heard a voice, "Puss, puss, puss . . . Mi-nou, Mi-nou, Mi-nou-nou-nou-nou."

"There you have it," Minou said. "He's calling me."

"Stay here," the Tatter Cat hissed. "Don't go to him. Don't give up your freedom. Next thing he'll be taking you to the vet in a basket . . . for a shot!"

Minou hesitated. "I think I'll go anyway," she said.

"You're mad," the Tatter Cat said. "Come with me. I know an old caravan at the back of a yard. . . . That'll be a roof over your head. You can take things easy while you turn back into a cat."

"Puss, puss, puss . . . Mi-nou!"

"I'm going," Minou said.

"No, stay here! Use your brain. If you have a litter, they'll drown your kittens."

"Puss, puss . . . Miss Minou!" the voice called.

"I'll come and visit," Minou said. "Here on the roof. Bye."

She jumped down to a lower level, nimbly climbed a sloping, tiled roof, and lowered herself down on the other side. Then she crawled along the gutter on all fours, grabbed her case, stood up, and stepped over in front of the kitchen window.

"Here I am," she said.

"Come in," said Tibble.

—4—
THE CAT PRESS AGENCY

"S it down, Tibble," the editor said.

Tibble sat down. It had been exactly one week since he had last sat on this chair, blinking in the light. It had been a very unpleasant conversation, but things were different now.

"I don't know what's got into you, Tibble," his boss said. "But you've changed a lot. Last week I almost kicked you out, you know that? I was going to fire you, I'd made up my mind. I guess it was pretty clear. Then I said I'd give you one last chance. And lo and behold! In this one week you've come up with all kinds of interesting news. You were the first to know about Mr. Smith and his anniversary. And you were the first to know about the new swimming pool. That was *secret*. But you *still* found out about it. . . . I can't help but wonder, how did you find out about that?"

"Well . . . ," Tibble said. "I talked to some people here and there."

"Some people here and there" was just Minou. And Minou had heard it from the Council Cat, who always sat in on the closed council meetings at the town hall.

"And that article about the hoard they found next to the church," his boss said. "A pot full of old coins buried in the churchyard! You didn't waste any time with that one either. You were the first on the scene yet again."

Tibble smiled modestly. One of the Tatter Cat's daughters had provided that bit of news. It had been the Church Cat, Ecumenica. And she herself had found the pot of old coins while scratching in the churchyard for simple toiletry reasons. Tibble had gone straight to the sexton and told him. And then he'd written an article about it.

"Keep it up, Tibble," his boss said. "You don't seem to be shy at all anymore."

Tibble blushed. It wasn't true . . . unfortunately. He was still as shy as ever. The news all came from the cats; he only needed to write it up. Although . . . he did often need to check that the things he'd heard were actually true. But usually a single phone call was enough to take care of that. "Excuse me, Mr. Whatever, I heard that so-and-so did this or that, is that true?" Up till now it had always been true. The cats hadn't told him any fibs.

And there were so many cats in Killenthorn. Every building had at least one. Now, at this very moment, there was one sitting on the windowsill in the editor's office.

It was the Editorial Cat. He blinked at Tibble.

That cat listens to everything, Tibble thought. I hope he doesn't tell nasty stories about me.

"And so," the editor continued, "I've been thinking of increasing your salary at the end of the month."

"Thank you, sir, great," Tibble said. He snuck a glance at the Editorial Cat and felt himself blushing again. There was a hint of cold contempt in the cat's eyes. He probably thought Tibble was groveling.

A little later, out on the street, where the sun was shining, Tibble felt a tremendous urge to run and skip; he was that relieved.

And when he saw someone he knew, he shouted out "Hello" at the top of his voice.

It was Bibi, a little girl who lived nearby and sometimes visited him in his attic.

"Would you like an ice cream?" Tibble asked. "Come on, I'll buy you an extra-large one."

Bibi was in Mr. Smith's class at school and told Tibble that they were having a drawing competition. She was going to do a really big picture.

"What are you going to draw?" Tibble asked.

"A cat," Bibi said.

"Do you like cats?"

"I love all animals." She licked her big pink ice cream.

"When you've finished your drawing, come and show it to me," Tibble said, and went home.

Minou had been living in his attic for a week now, and all things considered, it wasn't too bad. What it actually came down to was that he now had two cats instead of just one.

Minou slept in the box. And she did most of her sleeping in the daytime. At night she'd go out through the kitchen

window, then wander over the rooftops and through the back gardens, talking to the many cats in the surrounding area and not coming home to her box until early in the morning.

The most important thing was that she provided him with news. The first few days it had been Fluff who had busied himself searching for the latest stories. But Fluff wasn't a real news cat. He mostly came back with gossip about catfights, or boasting about a rat he'd smelt near the docks or a fish head he'd found somewhere. He wasn't really interested in human rumors.

No, the great source of news was the Tatter Cat. She knew everything.

That was mainly because she was a stray who swiped her meat scraps from all layers of society. And because she had an extensive family.

The Tatter Cat had children and grandchildren all over town.

Minou met her at night on the roof of the Social Security Building and always took a small bag of fish for her.

"Thanks," the Tatter Cat would say. "My daughter, the Council Cat, is waiting for you at the town hall. She's sitting on one of the marble lions out front and she's got some news for you. . . ."

Or "The Butcher's Cat wanted to tell you something. He's in the third garden on the left after the chestnut. . . ."

That same night Minou went down the Social Security Building fire escape, slunk over a courtyard, and slipped through a rear gate into an alley. And from there to the prearranged spot where some cat or other would be waiting.

"Soon we'll have to change our meeting spot," the Tatter Cat said. "My kids are going to be born in a few days, I can feel it, and then I'll have to stay close to the little monsters and won't be able to come up on the rooftops. But that won't matter. The message service will still work. All the cats have been informed. They know your human is waiting for news, and they're watching out for it. They're keeping their eyes peeled and their ears open. They'll pass it on."

"Where are you going to have your kittens?" Minou asked. "Have you found a good spot?"

"Not yet," the Tatter Cat said. "But I will."

"Can't you move in with us? In the attic?"

"Never!" the Tatter Cat cried. "I'll never give up my freedom! And stop nagging."

"My human's very nice," Minou said.

"I know. He's a good human, as far as that goes. . . . But I just don't like the species. They're not too bad until they grow up . . . some of them, at least. Do you know Bibi?"

"No."

"She's drawing me," the Tatter Cat said. "In detail! And she likes the way I look, even now, with this big gut. She thinks I'm beautiful! Can you believe it? Anyway, I'll let you know where I am when the time comes. Somewhere in town, close to a radio."

"Why close to a radio?"

"I like a bit of background music when I'm having kittens," the Tatter Cat said. "It makes it easier. And more cheerful. Remember that, if it ever happens to you."

* * *

When Minou came home with some news story or other and told Tibble how she'd got it, he cried, "It's all so organized! One cat passes it on to the next. . . . It's a kind of cat press agency."

"I'm not sure I like the sound of that," Minou said hesitantly. "A cat press . . . it makes me think of a garlic press. Squished cat."

"Not a *cat-press* agency," Tibble said, "a cat *press agency*."

The arrangement had saved him, and as far as he was concerned, things were going excellently.

Sometimes, when he came in, he'd find Minou in a corner of the room. She'd be crouched down on the floor, dead still and staring at a hole in the skirting board.

"Miss Minou! That's one more habit you have to break! Lying in wait at a mouse hole! That's not the kind of thing a lady does!"

She stood up and tried to get back into his good books by rubbing her head against his shoulder.

"That's not right either," Tibble sighed. "Real ladies don't rub up against people. At most they rub them up the wrong way. I wish you'd stop doing all these catty things."

"*Catty* is not the correct word," Minou said. "It's called *cattish*."

"Fine, cattish. But I feel like you're getting more and more cattish. It would be much better if you had more to do with people. Instead of just seeing cats all the time. You should go out on the rooftops less often and down on the street more—in the daytime."

"I don't dare, Mr. Tibble. I'm scared of people."

"Nonsense. People aren't scary at all!"

She looked at him for a moment with her slanting eyes, then turned away shyly.

How can I say something like that? he thought. When I'm so shy and scared myself? When I prefer the company of cats?

But he decided to stick to his guns.

"What's that I see!" he cried.

Minou was washing herself. She'd licked her wrist and was rubbing behind her ear with the wet spot.

"That takes the cake! Yuck!"

"It's—it's just . . . ," Minou stammered, "I was hoping it would make it go faster."

"Make what faster? Washing?"

"No, that's faster in the shower. I mean, turning into a cat. I still haven't given up hope that . . . I'd just prefer to be a cat again."

Tibble slumped down on the couch.

"Listen," he said. "I wish you'd stop all this nonsense. You never *were* a cat. It's all in your imagination. You dreamt it."

She didn't answer.

"Honestly," Tibble went on. "Absolute nonsense."

Minou yawned and stood up.

"What are you doing?"

"I'm going to get in my box," she said.

Fluff curled around her legs and, together with the gray

cat, she made her way over to the corner of the attic where she kept her box.

Tibble called after her in an angry voice, "If you *were* a cat . . . *whose* cat were you?"

No answer came. He heard a quiet, purring meow. A conversation in Cattish. Two cats talking behind the partition.

—5—

TIBBLE'S SECRETARY

One afternoon when Tibble was climbing the stairs to his attic, he heard a furious screeching coming from his flat; it sounded like two cats fighting.

He raced up the rest of the staircase three steps at a time and stormed into his living room.

He had a visitor. But it wasn't exactly a tea party.

Crouched on the floor was the little girl, Bibi. Minou was across from her, also on the floor. There was an empty box next to them, and they both had a hand on something. They were yelling at each other at the top of their lungs.

"What is it? What have you got there?" Tibble cried.

"Let go!" Bibi screamed.

"What's under your hands?" Tibble asked again. "*Miss Minou! Will you please let go immediately!*"

Minou looked up at him with an expression that was more cattish than ever.

There was a vicious, murderous glint in her eyes, and she refused to let go. She closed the hand with the small, sharp nails even tighter around whatever it was she was holding.

"Let go, I said!" Tibble smacked her hand, hard. She slid back and hissed furiously, but she did let go. In almost the same instant, though, she lashed out, clawing him painfully on the nose.

And now Tibble saw what it was: a white mouse. Still unharmed.

Gently Bibi picked up the mouse and put it back in its box, but she was crying from fright and indignation.

"It's *my* mouse," she sobbed. "I only got it out to show her, and then she jumped on it. I'm leaving. And I'm never coming back."

"Wait, Bibi, please," Tibble said. "Don't rush off. Listen. This is Miss Minou. She's, um . . . she's . . ." He thought for a moment. "She's my secretary and she doesn't mean any harm. Not at all. In fact, she really loves mice."

Minou was on her feet now and staring down at the closed box. You could tell she loved mice, but not the way Tibble meant.

"Isn't that right, Miss Minou?" Tibble asked. "You didn't want to hurt the poor mouse, did you?"

Minou leant over to rub her head against his shoulder, but he took a step to one side.

"What else have you got there, Bibi?" Tibble asked, pointing at a large collecting tin.

"I'm going round with the tin," Bibi said. "Collecting money.

35

It's for the present. The present for Mr. Smith's anniversary. And you've got blood on your nose."

Tibble wiped his nose with his hand. There was blood all over it.

"Don't worry about that," he said. "I'll put some money in your tin."

"And I've come to show you my drawing," Bibi said. She unrolled a big sheet of paper, and Tibble and Minou shouted out together, "That's the Tatter Cat! It looks just like her."

"It's for the drawing competition at school," Bibi said. "I just came by to show you."

"It's beautiful," Tibble said, and felt yet another drop of blood running down his face.

"If I go and look for a bandage in the bathroom," he said gruffly, "I hope that *you*, Miss Minou, will be able to control yourself for a moment." He put the mouse box on his desk, gave Minou a menacing look, and backed out of the room.

I've got a secretary, he thought. That sounds excellent, very posh. But she happens to be a secretary who wouldn't hesitate to gobble up a little girl's white mouse if she got a chance.

He hurried back into the living room with a crooked bandage on his nose and was surprised to discover that Minou and Bibi had become great friends in the meantime. The mouse box was still safe on his desk.

"Can I see the attic?" Bibi asked. "The whole attic?"

"Sure," Tibble said. "Look around. I've actually got two ca—I mean . . . I have a cat too. As well as a secretary. Um . . . he's called Fluff, but he's out on the roof. Miss Minou, would you show Bibi the rest of the attic? Then I'll get to work."

Sitting at his desk, he heard the two of them whispering in the junk room behind the partition. He was very glad that Minou had found a friend, and when Bibi finally left he said, "Drop in again, if you like."

"That'd be fun," Bibi said.

"Don't forget your tin. I put something in it."

"Oh, yeah," Bibi said.

"And don't forget your drawing either."

"Oh, yeah."

"And don't forget your box with the, um . . . *you-know-what* in it." He was too scared to say the word *mouse* in front of his secretary.

"Oh, yeah."

"And I hope you win first prize!" Tibble called after her.

Downstairs, in the house the attic belonged to, lived Mrs. Van Dam.

Fortunately Tibble had his own front door and his own staircase, so he didn't have to go through her house to come in or go out.

That afternoon, Mrs. Van Dam said to her husband: "Put that newspaper down for a second. I need to talk to you."

"What about?" her husband asked.

"About that upstairs neighbor of ours."

"Oh, you mean that young fellow? Tibble? What about him?"

"I don't think he's alone up there."

"What do you mean he's not alone?"

"I think he has a woman living with him."

"Oh," said Mr. Van Dam, "that must be nice for him." And he picked his newspaper up again.

"Yes, but I think it's a very *strange* young woman," his wife said.

"Either way, it's none of our business," he said.

It was quiet for a moment. Then she said, "She spends all her time up on the roof."

"Who?"

"The woman upstairs. At nighttime she goes out on the roof."

"How do you know?" Mr. Van Dam asked. "Do you go up on the roof at night to have a look?"

"No, but the lady across the road looks out of her attic window sometimes and she always sees her sitting there. With cats on both sides of her."

"You know I don't like gossip," Mr. Van Dam said irritably. He carried on reading while his wife went to the front door, because someone had rung the doorbell.

It was Bibi with her collecting tin.

"Would you like to make a donation for Mr. Smith's present?" she asked.

"I'd love to," said Mrs. Van Dam. "Come in and sit down for a moment."

Bibi sat on a chair with her legs dangling and the tin on her knee, the drawing under one arm and the mouse box next to her.

"Tell us, have you been upstairs yet? To the attic flat?" Mrs. Van Dam asked casually.

"Yes," Bibi said. "To Mr. Tibble and Miss Minou's."

"Miss Minou?" Mrs. Van Dam asked sweetly, putting a coin in the tin. "Who's that?"

"His secretary."

"Goodness."

"She sleeps in a box," said Bibi.

Now Mr. Van Dam looked up over his reading glasses. "In a box?"

"Yes, in a big cardboard box. She just fits. Curled up. And she always goes out through the window, onto the roof. And she talks to cats."

"Oh," said Mr. Van Dam.

"She can talk to all the cats," Bibi explained, "because she used to be one herself."

"Who says so?"

"She does. And now I have to go."

"Don't forget your tin," said Mrs. Van Dam. "And here, don't forget this roll of paper. And your box."

Once Bibi was gone, she said, "There. What did I tell you? Do we have a strange woman living upstairs or don't we?"

"She does sound a little odd," said Mr. Van Dam. "But I still think it's no concern of ours."

"Listen," she said. "When it comes down to it, it's *our* attic. Tibble rents the attic from *us*. And I have a right to know what's going on under *my* roof."

"What are you doing?" her husband asked.

"I'm going up there."

"Just like that? What are you going to say?"

"I don't know. I'll think of something."

Even though it was a warm spring day and she only had to take two steps out on the street, Mrs. Van Dam put on her fur coat.

She was going to ring the doorbell, but Bibi had left the front door open, so it wasn't necessary and she went straight up the stairs. It was a tall, steep staircase, and she was puffing in her thick fur coat.

"Hello, Mrs. Van Dam," said Tibble.

"Hello, Mr. Tibble. Sorry for barging in on you like this . . ."

"No problem at all, come in. Can I take your coat?"

"No, no. I'm not staying," Mrs. Van Dam said as she stepped into the living room.

There was no one there except Tibble.

"Haven't you made it lovely," she said, looking around everywhere. "And what a cute little kitchen . . . and that gorgeous view out over the roofs."

"Shall I make some tea?"

"No, thank you. I was really only popping in. I just wanted to tell you that I always read your articles in the paper. Lovely articles . . . And this must be the storage space. . . . You don't mind me having a look, do you?"

"There's only junk in there," Tibble said. "Old chairs and boxes. Things like that."

But she slipped past him, chattering cheerfully.

"Oh, I always love poking around in places like this!" she said. "Old corners of old attics."

Tibble tagged along helplessly behind her. Now she'd reached the big cardboard box and was bending over it. The movement made the floor creak under her weight.

Minou woke up. She opened one eye. Then she leapt up out of the box with a shriek.

Mrs. Van Dam recoiled in fright. Furious cat eyes glared at

40

her. A hand with sharp pink nails moved toward her and the creature *hissed*.

"Sorry . . . ," Mrs. Van Dam spluttered, backing up quickly. She turned to flee, but Tibble stopped her with a friendly gesture. "May I introduce you to my secretary, Miss Minou . . . and this is my downstairs neighbor, Mrs. Van Dam."

Mrs. Van Dam turned back nervously. The strange creature was just an ordinary young woman with a polite smile.

"Pleased to meet you," said Mrs. Van Dam.

"Won't you sit down for a moment?"

"No, no. I really must be going. It was lovely of you to show me round your flat."

She peered at the bandage on Tibble's nose for a moment and then said, "Bye."

After she'd left, Tibble let out a deep sigh and said, "This attic is hers. She's my landlady."

"How horrible!" Minou said.

"No, it's all right. What's horrible about it? I just pay the rent. And otherwise we don't have anything to do with her."

"That's not what I mean," Minou said. "I mean, how horrible . . . there must have been at least twenty."

"Twenty? Twenty what?"

"Cats."

"Twenty cats? Where?"

"In that coat . . . ," Minou said with a shudder. "That fur coat. I was lying there asleep in my box and suddenly I wake up with a start and there's twenty dead cats standing in front of me."

"Oh, that's why you hissed at her. You came this close to clawing her. You have to control yourself a little better, Miss

Minou. Clawing the landlady just because she's wearing a coat made of cat fur. Shame on you!"

"If she comes back I really will claw her," said Minou.

"Nonsense. She bought that coat in a shop, and when she bought it those cats were long dead. It's all because you don't mix enough with people. You spend too much time up on the rooftops. You don't get down to the streets enough."

"I was on the street last night."

"You have to get out in the *daytime*. Go out and do some shopping like other people."

"All right. But I'm waiting till dark," Minou said.

"No, the shops will be shut then. You have to go now."

"I wouldn't dare."

"We need bread and biscuits," Tibble continued.

"I'm too scared."

"And we've run out of fish. You could pop by the fishmonger's. He's got a stall on the corner of Green Square."

"Oh," said Minou. "Maybe I can learn to be brave enough. Once I'm out on the street."

"I'm sure of it," Tibble said. "You'll get better and better at it. Just . . ."

"What?"

"I'd prefer it if you didn't rub up against the fishmonger."

—6—

THE NEIGHBORHOOD

Minou walked down the street with a shopping basket over one arm.

Besides that first time when the dog treed her, she'd never seen this neighborhood in the daytime. She only really knew the town from the rooftops and in the dark. And she knew the back gardens better than the streets and squares.

She felt like slinking along and hiding behind parked cars and in doorways as she went, darting from one to the other. The people and traffic made her very uneasy.

"But I don't have to sneak around," she told herself. "I'm a human going out to do some shopping. Here comes a doggy. There's no need to get frightened; it's only a little dog . . . and I mustn't hiss at it. And I definitely shouldn't stop to sniff the rubbish bins. I'm going shopping, like all the other humans out and about in this part of town."

From very far away Minou smelt the fish stall on Green Square and started walking faster and faster to get there sooner.

And when she was almost there, she circled it a couple of times at a distance until she suddenly thought, I can *buy* some fish. I've got a purse. I don't need to beg and I don't need to steal. She went up to the fishmonger. He smelt delicious, and Minou slipped in a quick rub of her head against his shoulder. He didn't notice; he was too busy gutting fish.

She bought herring and mackerel, and lots of everything, and after she'd paid she brushed her head against the fishmonger's arm once again. He looked up with surprise, but Minou just strode off on her way to the baker's.

She passed Mr. Smith's school. The windows were open; she could hear children singing, and she could see the class sitting there. Bibi was there too.

Now a cat jumped up onto the school wall. It was the School Cat. "Nosey-nosey first," he said.

Minou pushed her nose forward and felt the School Cat's cold pink nose against it. This was how the cats here in town greeted each other when they weren't fighting.

"If you give me a piece of fish," the School Cat said, "I'll tell you some news for the paper."

Minou gave him some.

"Fantastic news," the School Cat said. "The Spanish Armada has been defeated. By Sir Francis Drake. Make sure they put it in the paper."

"Thanks," said Minou.

Two houses up sat Cross-Eyed Simon, Mr. Smith's Siamese.

"Give me a piece of fish," he said, "and I'll tell you something."

Once he had the piece in his claws, he said: "You should never listen to the School Cat. He always sits in on the history lessons. He thinks it's exciting and doesn't realize it all happened ages ago."

"I got that," Minou said. "But what did *you* want to tell me?"

"That," said Simon.

"You're all just after the fish," Minou said. "I'm glad I bought a lot."

Now she passed the factory. It was the deodorant factory. This was where they made spray cans with smells in them, and it stank of disgusting violets. Nowhere near as nice as the fish stall.

Minou was about to hurry past when the factory cat came up to her. The Deodorant Cat was one of the Tatter Cat's sons. He had a very strong smell of violets about him.

"I suppose you've got some news for me if I give you some fish," Minou said.

"How'd you guess?" the cat asked.

"You can have a piece of mackerel."

"Firstly," said the Deodorant Cat, "the nicest cafeteria boy in the whole factory just got fired. He's over there now. He's called Billy. It's a terrible shame because he was really kind to me and patted me every day."

"Why'd they fire him?" Minou asked.

"He was always too late."

"Oh, that's a shame," said Minou. "But it's not news for the paper."

"No? Fine, that was 'Firstly,' then. Now comes 'Secondly.' There are plans to expand our factory. I sat in on a secret meeting today. They're going to turn this whole neighborhood into one big perfume factory."

"That's real news," said Minou. "Thanks."

"But they don't have permission yet!" The cat called after her. "The councillor still has to approve it."

Minou hadn't bumped into many people during her shopping expedition, but she had met quite a few cats, and there were a few more on her way to the baker's.

The baker's wife was standing behind the counter, and there were already a couple of women in the shop. Minou waited politely for her turn, but while she was standing there looking around, Muffin the Bakery Cat came into the shop from the house, meowing loudly.

She's after my fish, thought Minou, but then she heard what Muffin was saying.

"*Meow, meow*! Now, now!" the cat cried. "Tell her now!"

Minou hurried up to the counter and said, "Your little boy Jack has got the kerosene bottle. Upstairs, in the bathroom."

The baker's wife looked at her with shock, dropped the bread rolls on the counter, and ran out of the shop without a word.

Minou felt the stares of the other customers. It was very intimidating, and she was about to hurry off when the baker's wife came back.

"It was true," she panted. "I got upstairs and there was my three-year-old, little Jack . . . with the kerosene bottle . . . pouring it out. . . . You can't leave them alone for a second. . . . Thank you so much for warning me."

Suddenly she stopped and looked at Minou.

"How did you know?" she asked. "You can't see into our bathroom from down here."

Minou was about to say, "Muffin told me," but then she saw the women staring at her. She stumbled over her words. "I . . . it was just a feeling."

"Well, thank you anyway. Whose turn is it?"

"The young lady can go first," said the other customers.

Minou asked for bread and biscuits and paid.

No sooner had she left the shop than they started talking behind her back.

"That's Mr. Tibble's young lady. . . ."

"She's his secretary . . . and she sleeps in a box. . . ."

"And she sits on the roof at night. . . ."

"A very strange young lady . . ."

"Well," said the baker's wife after listening to it all, "she may be strange, but she certainly did me a tremendous favor. End of story. A small loaf of brown, you said?"

Meanwhile Tibble was waiting.

More than an hour had passed since Minou went out to do some shopping. Just bread and fish, that couldn't take this long.

He sat at his desk, nervously chewing his nails. Just when he was starting to wonder whether he should go out to look for her, the phone rang.

"Hello," said Tibble.

"Hello, Mr. Tibble, this is Mrs. Van Dam speaking. From downstairs, you know. I'm calling from a phone box. Your secretary is up a tree. And she can't get down again."

"Oh, thank you very much," Tibble said.

"You're welcome."

Too late he shouted, "Which tree?" But she'd already hung up.

"Here we go again!" Tibble cried. "What a pain!" And he ran down to the street.

Green Square first, that was where most of the trees were. When he arrived, he saw where she was at once. There was a large group of people gathered round. It wasn't the same tree as last time; it was another one that was even taller. Bibi was there too because school had just finished for the day.

"A dog chased her," Bibi said.

"Uh-huh," sighed Tibble. He wasn't surprised. "How do we get her back down again?"

"The fishmonger's already at it," Bibi said. "He's up in the tree. He's helping her down."

Amid great interest, the fishmonger helped Minou down through the branches. First onto the roof of the greengrocer's van, then down onto the street.

"Thank you very much," she said, sniffing at his sleeve one last time. "Oh, my basket must be here somewhere."

Tibble picked it up. There were biscuits and bread in it and a little bit of fish.

"We have to do something about it," Tibble said when they were back home. "Things really can't go on like this, Miss Minou."

She was sitting in the corner looking very repentant.

"It was the same dog again," she said. "He's called Mars."

"It's not just getting stuck in trees," Tibble said. "It's all these cattish traits. . . . You have to stop acting like that."

"Being rescued by the fishmonger was lovely," Minou said wistfully.

That annoyed Tibble even more, but before he could say anything she blurted, "Oh, yeah, I heard some news too while I was out." She told him about the expansion of the perfume factory. It calmed him down a little; he had something new to write about.

— 7 —

"YOUR SISTER CAME BY"

When Minou went up on the roof that night, the Tatter Cat wasn't there. Instead there was another cat waiting for her. The School Cat.

"She says hi," he said. "She couldn't make it."

"Have the kittens arrived?"

"Seventeen or so, I think," said the School Cat.

"Where are they?"

"You know the parking lot behind the gas station? It's best to stick to the gardens until you get to the big hawthorn, then go through the hedge. There are a couple of abandoned campers there. She's moved into one of them. Temporarily."

"I'll go straight there," said Minou.

"Give me some fish before you go."

"It's not for you, it's for the Tatter Cat. I've got some milk with me too."

"I don't want any milk. If you give me a piece of fish I'll tell you some news. For the paper."

Minou gave him a tiny piece.

"Guy Fawkes tried to blow up the Houses of Parliament," the School Cat said. "Make sure it's in tomorrow's paper."

"Thanks," said Minou. He'd been sitting in on the history lesson again.

She passed through shadowy gardens to the garage where they repaired cars in the daytime. The garage was closed, but the petrol station was open; it was all lit up and they had the radio on. All night long.

It seemed the Tatter Cat had got what she wanted. Background music.

The parking lot behind the gas station was dark. And very quiet. There were a few overnight cars and right at the back there was a row of campers.

An ordinary person would have found it difficult to find their way on such a dark night, but Minou, with all her cattish traits, had excellent eyesight and easily found the Tatter Cat's home.

It was an old, run-down camper. There was a broken window with a curtain flapping in the wind and the door was half open. Inside, the Tatter Cat was lying on an old blanket on the floor. Under her, a tangle of kittens.

"Six of them!" she cried indignantly. "*Six!* Unbelievable. What did I do to deserve something like this? Can you see them? Get out from under me, you riffraff!" she said to the babies. "Look, now you can see them better. There's *one* ginger.

51

He's a dead ringer for his dad, the Pump Cat. And the rest are all tortoiseshells, like me. And now give me something to eat. I'm dying of hunger."

Minou knelt down next to her and looked at the six writhing kittens.

They had tiny little tails and blind eyes and teensy little claws. In the distance the radio was playing.

"Hear it?" the Tatter Cat asked. "Cozy, huh? It's all modern conveniences here."

"Is it safe?" Minou asked. "Whose camper is it?"

"Nobody's. It's been empty for years. Nobody ever comes here. Did you see the Pump Cat around anywhere?"

"No."

"He hasn't been here *once* to see his children," the Tatter Cat said. "Not that I want him hanging round the place, but still! And now give me that fish. You've got milk too. In a bottle. Are you expecting me to drink out of a bottle?"

"Be quiet now. I've brought a saucer."

While the mother cat lapped up the milk, Minou looked around. "I wouldn't feel at ease here," she said. "A parking lot, that means people. Lots of people in the daytime."

"We're in a quiet corner," the Tatter Cat said.

"But your children would be much safer in Mr. Tibble's attic."

The Tatter Cat made an angry gesture that sent her kittens sprawling and set off a chorus of pathetic squeaking.

"Shut your traps!" their mother roared. "They just guzzle away all day and all night. And the least little thing has 'em screaming blue murder!"

Then she shot Minou a vicious glare through the dark with

her burning yellow eyes. And she hissed, "If you take my kids away, I'll scratch your eyes out."

"Take them away? I'd take you too, of course."

"Thanks for the offer, but I'm fine right here."

"Later, when they're bigger, I could look for homes for them."

"No need. They'll make their own way. Let 'em become strays, like me. They should steer clear of humans. I always say there are two kinds of human. One kind's nasty lowlife skunks."

She was quiet for a moment and took a big bite of poached fish.

Minou waited patiently.

"And the other kind?" she asked.

"I've forgotten the other kind," the Tatter Cat said. "*Erk-erk-erk-erk* . . ." A gagging sound came up out of her throat.

Minou patted her on her skinny shoulders and the Tatter Cat spat out a fish bone.

"Just what I needed," she said. "Choking on a stupid bone. Be a bit careful next time you bring me some fish, will you? I've got enough problems as it is with this whole kitten nursery hanging off me. But you know what's so great here? I'm really close to all those posh gardens. Because just over there"—she waved one paw—"it's all big fancy houses."

"They have dogs at big fancy houses," said Minou.

"Sometimes, but if you're lucky they keep 'em chained up. And the blackbirds in those gardens are as fat as the ladies who live in the houses. And in weather like this, they always leave the garden doors open. You can sneak in and there's always something to nick. It'd actually be better if *you* came to live here with *me*. Why not? There's plenty of room. We can go hunting together! And I'm sure, very sure, that if you ate a nice fat thrush, you'd soon turn back into a respectable cat again—that's right!"

"What's the matter?"

"I'm such a moron," the Tatter Cat said. "I forgot there was something I had to tell you. . . . All this maternal love has gone to my head."

"That's OK. Tell me now."

"It's not for the paper. It's a personal message for you. Your aunt was here. Your aunt Sooty. She wanted to talk to you, but she's too old to go up on the rooftops, and that's why she left the message with me."

"What did she want?"

"She asked if you'd drop by. She's had a visit from your sister."

Minou jumped. "My . . . my sister? But she lives miles away. Right out on the other side of town. What was she doing here?"

"Take it easy," said the Tatter Cat. "That's all I know. I'm as *purrplexed* as you. Ha-ha, good joke, huh? And when you come tomorrow, make sure you get all the bones out of the fish first."

"Is it all right if I bring my human to visit? Just once?" Minou asked. "And Bibi?"

"Bibi's OK," the Tatter Cat said without hesitating. "She drew me. Have you seen it?"

"It's a beautiful likeness," said Minou.

"But I don't know about Tibble . . . I'm scared he'll start fussing," said the Tatter Cat. "He's a fusser. Even worse than you. He'll want to take my babies away . . . arrange vets and shots and looking for homes . . . all that . . ."

"I'll tell him he's not allowed to make a fuss," Minou said. "See you tomorrow."

54

* * *

On the way home she took a detour through Aunt Sooty's garden. She stayed in among the shrubs, but as soon as she let out a short meow, her elderly aunt came out through the cat flap.

"You haven't made much progress," Aunt Sooty said disapprovingly. "No tail, no whiskers, and you're still wearing that horrible two-piece suit."

"I heard—" Minou began.

"Yes, yes," Aunt Sooty interrupted her. "Your sister was here."

Minou trembled and her voice was a little hoarse when she asked, "My sister from Victoria Avenue?"

"Yes, of course it was the one from Victoria Avenue," Aunt Sooty said. "You don't have any other sisters, do you?"

"She chased me away," said Minou. "Out of the house and out of the garden. She was angry at me. Because I wasn't a cat anymore. I wasn't allowed to come back, ever, that's what she said. "

"Quite understandable." Aunt Sooty nodded. "But she says hello. She's not angry anymore. She feels sorry for you."

"Can I go back?" Minou asked. "Does she want me back?"

"Not like you are now!" Aunt Sooty exclaimed. "First you have to turn back into a respectable cat, obviously."

"It was such a lovely garden on Victoria Avenue," Minou said. "It was my own garden and my own house . . . and our Woman was kind to us. Do you think the Woman would want me back?"

"Of course she would, as long as you're normal again," Aunt Sooty said. "And shall I let you in on a secret? Your sister has

55

found out where it came from. This . . . condition of yours. She had the same thing."

"*What?*" Minou cried. "Is she—"

"Shhh . . . not so loud," Aunt Sooty said. "No, she isn't . . . but almost. She started getting human traits too. Her whiskers fell out. . . . Her tail began to disappear. . . . It was all because you ate out of the rubbish bin at the institute. That's what your sister says."

"Is that what caused it?" Minou asked. "That was the building next door to our house in Victoria Avenue. . . . There was always a rubbish bin outside. And sometimes I found something to eat in it."

"Exactly," said Aunt Sooty. "You ate more of it than your sister. She got over it."

"Just like that? Did it go away of its own accord?"

"No, she says she found some kind of cure . . . something that made her normal again. But if you want to know the details, you have to drop by."

"Oh," said Minou.

"And if I were you, I'd do it sooner rather than later," said Aunt Sooty. "It's gone on long enough. What are you waiting for?"

"I'm not a hundred percent sure I want to," said Minou.

"You're mad!" Aunt Sooty cried. "Your one chance, your last chance to turn back into a proper cat. And you're not sure you want to!"

"I'm umming and aahing," said Minou.

Aunt Sooty went back into the house in a huff and Minou went home, to her own roof, where she sat down to watch the moon rise over the Social Security Building. The smell of blossoms rose up from the gardens far below, and in the gutters around the roofs there were all kinds of cat smells. It was very confusing.

The next morning Tibble gave her a package.

"A present," he said. "Because I've had a pay raise."

"How beautiful, thank you," said Minou. It was a pair of gloves.

"They're for the reception," explained Tibble.

"The reception?"

"There's a reception this afternoon at the Metropole Hotel. To celebrate Mr. Smith's anniversary. And I'd like you to come with me, Miss Minou. A lot of people will be coming."

"Then I don't want to," said Minou.

"It would be very good for you," said Tibble. "And for me too. We're both shy and we both have to Learn to Dare. I think the fishmonger will be there too."

"Oh," said Minou.

"I bought the gloves," Tibble said, "because I thought, then, if you scratch someone, it won't be so bad."

—8—

MR. SMITH'S RECEPTION

"**I** think I'd rather go back home," Minou said. "I'm scared."

They were on Green Square in front of the Metropole Hotel, where the reception for Mr. Smith was being held. There were a lot of cars out front, and people were streaming into the hotel.

Minou was wearing her new gloves, but now that she'd seen how busy it was, she felt very nervous.

"Don't be afraid," Tibble said. "Look, there's Bibi coming out of the hotel."

Bibi skipped up to them with a beaming smile on her face.

"What have you got there?" Tibble cried. "A camera!"

"First prize," said Bibi. "I won first prize in the drawing competition."

"And rightly so!"

"It's hanging on the wall," Bibi said. "In the reception room. They've hung up all our drawings. And they let me help present the gift."

"Are you going back in again?" Minou asked.

Bibi shook her head. "This afternoon is for grown-ups," she said. "We've already had our party. At school."

She walked on and Tibble said, "Come on, Miss Minou, let's go in. And remember! No purring, no hissing and don't rub up against anyone, not even the fishmonger."

"There won't be any dogs, will there?" Minou asked anxiously.

"No. Dogs don't come to receptions."

Inside, it was extremely crowded. Mr. Smith and his wife were sitting on a raised platform with floral arrangements left and right, and the children's drawings were on the wall behind them. It was a lovely exhibition, and the picture of the Tatter Cat was hanging in pride of place with a card saying *First Prize* next to it.

"Ah, look!" cried Mr. Smith. "There's Tibble. My dear Tibble, I'm so pleased you could make it. Look at the present I got from all the people in the neighborhood. A color TV! Isn't that fantastic?"

Tibble shook Mr. Smith's hand and said, "This is my secretary, Miss Minou."

"How do you do?" said Mr. Smith. "I believe I've seen you before, haven't I? In a tree . . ."

Other people came up to shake his hand and congratulate him, and Tibble and Minou walked on. All round the room there were groups of people gathered together to talk. There was the fishmonger. He waved at Minou and she blushed. The baker's wife nodded hello as well, and Minou started to feel more and more at ease.

It's going well, thought Tibble with a sense of relief. She's not cattish at all today.

Mrs. Van Dam was there too, in her fur coat, talking to a few other ladies, who nudged each other and looked in their direction.

Minou started getting nervous again. "Just ignore them," said Tibble.

They came to a table with all kinds of delicious snacks on it. Pieces of sliced sausage on toothpicks. And blocks of cheese on toothpicks.

"Can you just help yourself?" Minou asked.

"Later," said Tibble.

Now a large man wearing glasses and a pin-striped suit came in.

The room fell silent. Everyone bowed their heads low and respectfully in greeting.

"Is that the mayor?" Minou whispered.

"No," Tibble whispered back. "It's the owner of the factory, Mr. Ellmore. He's really important. And he does a lot of good."

"What's he do that's good?" Minou asked.

"He gives money to all kinds of charities."

Minou had more questions, but people around them had started going "Shhhh."

"Mr. Ellmore's about to speak," they said. Everyone pushed forward to listen, and Minou and Tibble got separated in the crowd.

Tibble was pushed over to one side, while Minou was jostled all the way to the front, close to the small table behind which Mr. Ellmore was giving his speech.

"Mr. Smith," he began, "ladies and gentlemen . . ."

Everyone was quiet.

"I am delighted to see so many people here this afternoon. . . ."

Mr. Ellmore was holding his car key in one hand and swung it gently back and forth over the table while speaking.

He swung it gently back and forth over the table.

Tibble looked at Minou and saw to his shock that her eyes were moving from side to side like at a tennis match. She wasn't listening at all; she was just staring intently at the swinging key, like a cat that's seen something move.

She's about to cuff it, thought Tibble, and he coughed very loudly, but she didn't notice.

"Many among us were once taught by Mr. Smith . . . ," the speaker continued. "And we all—"

Whack.

Minou's gloved hand smacked the key and sent it clattering over the table.

Mr. Ellmore was dumbstruck and stared at Minou with astonishment. All the people around her glared. Now she looked like a trapped cat searching for an escape route. Tibble tried to push forward, but all of a sudden she dived down and disappeared among the skirts and legs as she headed for the big table covered with snacks. She was gone.

Fortunately Mr. Ellmore resumed his speech, and the listening people soon forgot the incident.

Tibble snuck glances left and right and tried to look under the table. Had she crept in under it?

Now the speech was over and Mr. Smith gave a few words of thanks. Then waiters came round with trays of drinks and people began eating the snacks. Tibble moped around between the drinking, mingling groups. Where was she?

Maybe she'd slipped out of the door without anyone seeing? Minou was very good at slinking around and tiptoeing and slipping away unnoticed. Maybe she was home in the attic, in her box.

Tibble sighed. It had all gone so well. She hadn't hissed at anyone and she hadn't scratched anyone ... she hadn't even rubbed up against the fishmonger. But now she'd come up with something new. Another cattish trait.

He decided to stay a little longer.

Minou hadn't gone home. She was still in the hotel. She'd made it through a door without anyone noticing and now she was in another room. A smaller room, a kind of conference room. There was a table with chairs, a big planter box in one corner with lots of plants in it, and a goldfish bowl on a cabinet.

She was alone in the room, and she walked straight over to the fishbowl. Two fat goldfish were swimming around in slow circles with gulping mouths and bulging eyes. Completely at ease, swishing their tails now and then.

Minou bent over the fishbowl.

"This is really not allowed," she said to herself. "It's so cattish. In a moment I won't be able to control myself. Leave now, Minou. . . . Turn around."

But the fish were magnets. Two golden magnets tugging on her eyes. All by itself, her right hand with the beautiful long glove reached out to the bowl, just above it and—

Voices sounded close by and she pulled her hand back *just* in time. *Just* in time, she hid behind the planter box, because the door opened and two people came in.

One was Mr. Smith. The other was Mr. Ellmore.

Minou crouched down behind the ferns and creepers and didn't make a sound.

"I was hoping to speak to you for a moment," Mr. Smith said. "It's so busy in there, and nice and quiet here. This is what it's about: we, the local residents, would like to set up an association. The Animal Lovers' Association."

Ah, thought Minou behind the plants. News for Mr. Tibble. I'd better listen carefully.

"You know that there are an awful lot of animal lovers here in Killenthorn," Mr. Smith said. "Almost everyone has a cat. The aim of our association is to help as many animals as possible. We want to set up a home for poor stray cats, we'd like an animal hospital . . . and we hope to show films about animals. I myself," Mr. Smith continued, "am busy preparing a public reading about cats. It's going to be called 'The Cat Through the Ages: A Feline History.'"

More news, thought Minou.

"And I wanted to ask you," Mr. Smith said, "if you would be willing to be the president of our Animal Lovers' Association."

"Hm . . . ," said Mr. Ellmore. "Why *me*?"

"You're so well known," Mr. Smith said. "And you're so popular here in town. You're also a known animal lover. You have a cat yourself, I believe."

"I have a dog," said Mr. Ellmore. "Mars."

Minou started to quake so violently in her corner that the plants began shaking too. *Mars!* That was the dog that had treed her twice already.

"Hm . . . ," Mr. Ellmore said again. "Of course I'd *love* to do it, but you see . . . I'm so terribly busy. I'm already in so many associations and on so many committees. I'm already president of the Child Welfare Commission. . . ."

"It won't involve a lot of work," Mr. Smith said. "You won't need to do very much. It's more about your name. Everyone has so much faith in you."

Mr. Ellmore walked across the room and back again with his hands behind his back. He came very close to the planter box, looked at the goldfish for a moment, and then peered at the plants for what seemed like a very long time.

He can see me, thought Minou.

But he just pulled a dry leaf off a geranium and said, "Well, all right, then."

"Wonderful, wonderful!" cried Mr. Smith. "Thank you very much. We'll be in touch. Now I'd better get back to my party."

They left the room and Minou dared to breathe again.

She came out and saw an enormous black tom sitting on the ledge of the open window. It was the Hotel Cat. The Metropole Cat.

"That room's off-limits," the cat said. "I'm not allowed in there. Because of the fish. Did you see them?"

"I almost caught one," Minou said. "I have to go back to that room with all the people . . . but I'm scared."

"Your human's looking for you," the Metropole Cat said.

64

"Out front, on the terrace. If you climb out through the window you can go round the side. Then you won't need to go through the people."

With a little leap Minou was outside.

"Bye," she said, and walked around to the front, where Tibble was pacing back and forth.

"Miss Minou . . . ," he began in a strict voice.

"I've got some more news," she said.

She told him what she'd overheard and Tibble nodded gratefully.

But when they were back home in the attic, he said, "I think you really need to do something about it . . . all these cattish traits . . . this cattish behavior of yours. . . ."

"What can I do about it?"

"You have to go see a doctor."

"I don't want to," said Minou. "Doctors give you shots."

"No, I don't mean an ordinary doctor."

"What do you mean? An animal doctor?"

"No, I mean a head doctor. The kind of doctor you talk to when you have problems."

"I don't have any problems," said Minou.

"*I* do," said Tibble.

"Then *you* should go to a head doctor."

"My problems are caused by you, Miss Minou. By your strange habits. It was going so well this afternoon at the reception. You were behaving yourself perfectly . . . until you suddenly whacked that key ring with your paw—I mean, with your hand. Secretaries don't do things like that."

—9—

THE HEAD DOCTOR

And so the next day Minou found herself sitting in Dr. Gilt's office.

"Perhaps you can start by telling me your name," the doctor said, holding a pen over a card for his files.

"Minou."

MINOU, he wrote down. "Is that your first name? Or your surname?"

"It's the name they gave me."

"Ah, Minou is your given name. What's your family name?"

She was silent for a very long time, watching a fly buzz past the window. Then she said, "I don't think I have one."

"Really? What's your father's name?" the doctor asked, holding his pen ready again.

Minou thought for a moment, trying to remember, then said quietly, "He was a tom . . ."

TOM, wrote the doctor.

"At the back of a house . . ."

BACKHOUSE . . .

"Near one of the parks."

PARKES . . .

"Tom Backhouse-Parkes," said the doctor, reading what he'd noted down. "That's your name too then. Miss M. Backhouse-Parkes. Now tell me, what's bothering you?"

"Bothering me?" Minou asked. "Nothing's bothering me at all."

"But you wanted to see me. You must have had some reason."

"My human sent me."

"Your what?"

"My human, the Man I live with. He says I'm too cattish."

"Too what?"

"Too cattish. And he says I keep getting more and more cattish."

"Does he mean perhaps that you bear some resemblance to a cat?"

"Exactly," Minou said.

"Well," said the doctor. "Let's start at the beginning. Tell me a little about your parents. What did your father do?"

"He was a stray," Minou said. "I never knew him. I can't tell you anything about him."

"And your mother?"

"My mother was a tabby."

"Pardon?" The doctor looked at her over his glasses.

"She was a tabby. She's dead. They had her put to sleep."

"Mother, dead. Happened in her sleep," the doctor mumbled, and wrote it down.

"Not *happened* in her sleep, they *had her* put to sleep," Minou said.

"How terrible," the doctor said.

"Yes, there was nothing they could do. She'd been hit by a car. Blinded by the lights, but it was a long time ago."

"Well, carry on. Brothers or sisters?"

"There were five of us."

"And you were the eldest?"

"All five of us were the same age."

"Quintuplets? You don't get many of them."

"Course you do," said Minou. "Common as dirt. They gave away three of us when we were six weeks old. I was left over with my sister. The woman thought we were the cutest."

She smiled tenderly at the memory, and in the silence that followed the doctor clearly heard her purring. It sounded very peaceful. He was a great cat lover. He had one himself, Jemima, upstairs in his apartment.

"The woman?" he asked. "Was that your mother?"

"No," Minou said. "The Woman was our human. She said I had the most adorable tail."

"Aha," said the doctor. "And when did you lose it?"

"Lose what?"

"Your tail."

She gazed pensively at him, looking so much like a cat that he started to think, Oh, maybe she's still got one. Maybe it's curled up under her skirt.

"I ate something out of a rubbish bin," Minou said. "An *institute's* rubbish bin. That's what did it. But I've still got loads of cattish traits. I purr and I hiss. And I climb up into a tree when I see a dog."

"And is that a problem? Does it bother you?"

"Not me," Minou said. "But my human finds it unbecoming."

"Who's your human?"

"Mr. Tibble from the paper. I'm his secretary. It's all going very well, but I still feel one hundred percent cat."

"And is that a problem?" the doctor asked again.

"Things do get complicated," Minou said. "And sometimes it's very confusing being two creatures at the same time. Half cat and half human."

"Ah . . . ," said the doctor. "Sometimes it's very confusing being *all* human."

"Really?"

"Absolutely."

Minou had never thought of that. She found it an interesting idea. "Still, I'd rather just be one or the other," she said.

"And which would you prefer?"

"That's just it . . . I wish I knew. I can't make up my mind. Sometimes I think I'd be so glad to be a cat again. . . . Creeping under the golden chain tree with your tail up and the flowers brushing over your fur . . . and singing on the rooftops with the other cats and hunting in a garden when the young starlings have just left the nest. Sometimes I even miss the tray. Scratching in the kitty litter. But on the other hand . . . being a lady has advantages too."

"You'll just have to wait and see how it turns out," said the doctor.

"I thought . . . ," Minou said. "Maybe you can give me a mixture. Or drops. Something to . . ."

"Something to what? Turn you back into a cat?"

"No," said Minou. "I can't make up my mind."

"Well, when you have," the doctor said, "come back here. I don't have any mixtures or drops for you, but talking always helps."

There was a scratching at the door. It was the Doctor's Cat, Jemima.

"My cat wants to come in," the doctor said, "but she knows she's not allowed in here when I have a patient."

Minou listened for a moment to the meowing on the other side of the door.

"You're wanted upstairs," she said. "Your wife is grilling some chicken."

"How do you know we're having chicken?" the doctor asked.

"And she's just burnt her thumb on the grill. . . . You're needed up there right away," Minou said. "I'll be off, then, Doctor, and I'll come back when I know what I want."

The doctor ran upstairs to his apartment. His wife had a big blister on her thumb and she was furious at the grill.

"How did you know something had happened?" she asked.

"A very charming cat told me," the doctor said, and went to get some ointment.

On her way home Minou heard the horrible news about the Tatter Cat. Cross-Eyed Simon told her.

"That's terrible," Minou said. "Her leg, you say? Broken? Was it a car? And where is she now? Are her children alone?"

"Don't ask so many questions at once," said Simon. "Maybe it's not as bad as it sounds. I heard it from the Pump Cat, and he always exaggerates. Someone hit her."

"Hit her?"

"That's right, with a bottle. And she only just managed to drag herself home to the caravan and her babies."

"I'll go straight there," said Minou. "I'll just get some food and milk for her first."

She found the Tatter Cat in the caravan with her kittens, surlier and angrier than ever.

"What happened?" Minou asked, kneeling down next to the blanket. "Is it bad? Is your leg broken? Are you bleeding?"

"They've crippled me," said the stray. "With a bottle of wine. A full one. No holding back there! Have you ever heard the likes? Maybe I should feel honored to get bashed with a bottle of burgundy!"

"Let me feel if anything's broken," said Minou.

"Don't touch me!" screeched the Tatter Cat.

"I just wanted to check it."

"Well, don't! Keep your hands to yourself."

"But if you've broken a leg, surely we need to do something about it."

"I'll get over it. It's all part of the game."

"But I could take you somewhere . . . up to our attic."

"I don't want to be taken anywhere. I'd rather die. I'm fine right here."

Minou sighed and gave the Tatter Cat some milk and some meat.

"Just in time," said the cat. "I was dry as a bone. I always drink

71

from the tap in the parking lot. There's a puddle under it. But it's on the other side of the parking lot and I can hardly walk."

When she'd had enough to drink, she said, "It was my own stupid fault."

"Tell me what happened."

"I'm walking through those posh gardens," said the Tatter Cat, "when I go past that big white house with all the roses. Mostly I'm too scared to go into their garden 'cause they've got a dog. But this time they've got him shut up in the garage. He's barking like crazy, but I just ignore him because he can't get to me anyway. The french doors are open, and I smell some very tasty smells inside. And I was hungry. Because with six of these squeaky little worms you stay hungry, take it from me. Anyway, I look in. And there's nobody in the room. But there is a big table set with food and a bunch of roses. I couldn't care less about the roses, of course, but I smelt salmon. So what do you do? You seize the opportunity."

"You went in?"

"Of course I went in. I jumped up on the table and landed with my feet right there in the salmon. And then I saw how much more there was! Lobster and chicken and sliced beef. Cream and shrimps and little bowls with all kinds of sauces. And all kinds of mashes and mushes . . . *Mrwah!*" The Tatter Cat drooled all over her babies.

"And then?"

"And then! It made my head spin, it was incredible. I was dizzy from all that food. I didn't know what to start on first. Idiot that I was. If I'd just eaten some of the salmon, at least I'd have had something. But those smells went to my head.

And now I can't believe I let the chance go by. I didn't have a single bite. *Mreeuw!*"

"Go on, what happened?"

"What do you think? All of a sudden there they were."

"Who?"

"The humans. The man and the woman. I hadn't heard them come in. Stupid, but . . . it was like I was drunk. I dived off the table and tried to get out through the french doors, but *she* was standing there with an umbrella and took a swing at me. So I shot back in the other direction, but that's where *he* was. He'd grabbed a full bottle of wine off the table. And *that* hurt! *Mrwowow!*" the Tatter Cat whimpered.

"How did you get out of there?"

"Don't ask me. I got out, that's for sure. I think I skidded past her legs and got a whack of the umbrella too, but I'm not sure about that. I shot into the garden. At first I didn't notice anything, but when I tried to jump over the hedge . . . something was wrong. I couldn't jump anymore. I couldn't climb either."

"How'd you get over it?" Minou asked.

"The dog. They let the dog out of the garage. I heard him coming. He was getting close and there weren't any holes in the hedge. None at all. I thought, you've had it now, old Tatter Cat. Crippled and up against a dog like that . . . You haven't got a chance. But I clawed him on the nose and that made him back up for a moment. And when the horrible thing attacked again, I suddenly thought of my litter of babies here, and that got me up over the hedge. *How* I don't know, but I made it."

"And how's walking going now?" Minou asked.

"Lousy. I just drag myself around at a snail's pace. But I'll get over it. It's all part of the game. That's the life of a stray. Anyway, at least I'm glad I gave that disgusting dog a scratch he won't forget in a hurry."

"What's the dog called?" Minou asked.

"Mars."

"What?"

"Oh, you know him, do you?"

"I know him," Minou said, ". . . but then it must have been his owner who hit you?"

"Yes, of course, that's what I'm telling you. Ellmore, he's called. He's the owner of the Deodorant Factory. Where my son, the Deodorant Cat, lives."

"He's also the president of an association," said Minou. "The Animal Lovers' Association."

"And there you have it," the Tatter Cat mocked. "The same old story, no surprise there. Humans . . . they're all scum."

"That's terrible," Bibi said after hearing the story. "What a horrible man. The poor Tatter Cat."

"You should go visit her," Minou said. "You know where she is."

"Yes, I've already been there once. In the old camper. Do you think she'd mind if I took a few photos of her babies?"

Bibi took her camera with her everywhere and was constantly snapping photos. The pictures were mostly very crooked, but they were all in focus.

Bibi and Minou had become good friends. Now they were sitting together on a bench in the park.

"Did Tibble put it in the paper?" Bibi asked. "I mean, about Mr. Ellmore and the Tatter Cat?"

"No," Minou said. "He's not allowed to write about cats. That's what he said."

"But this isn't just about cats! It's about the . . . the president of . . . what was it called again?"

"The Animal Lovers' Association."

"Well, that should go straight in the paper. A man like that crippling a poor mother cat."

"Yes, I think so too," said Minou, "but Tibble doesn't want to."

She looked past Bibi at the low-hanging branch of an elm. Bibi followed her gaze. A little bird was sitting there, singing. Bibi turned back to Minou and was shocked. . . . There was a very unpleasant look in her eye . . . just like that time with the mouse. . . .

"Minou!" Bibi screamed.

Minou jumped.

"I didn't do anything," she said. But she had a very guilty expression on her face.

"It's absolutely not allowed, remember that," Bibi said. "Birds are just as nice as cats."

"When I used to live in Victoria Avenue . . . ," Minou said dreamily.

"When you lived where?"

"Victoria Avenue. As a cat. I used to catch birds. . . . Behind the house, next to the patio, there was a golden chain tree. . . . That's where I caught most of them, and they were so . . ."

"I'm not listening anymore," Bibi shouted, running off with her camera.

75

—10—

CATS AREN'T WITNESSES

"I don't understand," Minou said for the umpteenth time. "This *has* to go in the paper: *Tatter Cat Crippled by the President of the Animal Lovers' Association.*"

"No," said Tibble. "'Cats aren't news,' that's what my boss says."

"Hitting a poor old mother cat with a bottle!" said Minou. "She might never recover."

"I'm not entirely surprised," Tibble said hesitantly, "at someone losing their temper when they suddenly see a stray cat standing on their salmon. And I *can* imagine them grabbing whatever's at hand to knock it off the table."

"Really?" said Minou, giving Tibble such a vicious look that he stepped back out of range of her nails.

"In any case, it's not something for the paper," he said. "And that's all there is to it."

Whenever Minou was angry, she got into her box to sulk. She was about to do that now, but Fluff came in through the kitchen window with a long-drawn-out meow.

"What's he saying?" Tibble asked.

"The fishmonger?" cried Minou.

"*Rwo . . . wwieeu . . . row . . .*," Fluff continued. He told her an ecstatic story in Cattish, then disappeared again, back on the roof.

"What about the fishmonger?" Tibble asked.

"He's in the hospital!"

"Really? I thought it sounded like Fluff had good news."

"The fishmonger got hit by a car," Minou said. "It ran right into his fish stall. All the local cats are going straight there because there's fish spread all over the road."

"I'm on my way," Tibble said. "I can write an article about this." And he grabbed his pad.

"I'm going too," Minou said. "Over the roof, that's faster."

She tried to climb out of the window, but Tibble stopped her. "No, Miss Minou. I don't want my secretary scrounging around an upset fish stall like an old alley cat!"

Minou gave him a haughty look.

"What's more," said Tibble, "there's bound to be a lot of people there, and you don't like that."

"Fine, I'll stay here," said Minou. "I'll hear the news on the roof."

* * *

There *were* a lot of people in Green Square. A real crowd. The police were there, there was glass on the street from the broken windows, and the fish stall was completely wrecked; there were slats and boards all over the place, the bunting had been trodden underfoot, and the last cat was running off with the last herring.

Mr. Smith was looking around too.

"They just drove off with the fishmonger," he said. "They're taking him to the hospital. He's got a broken rib."

"What happened?" Tibble asked.

"A car! But the weird thing is nobody knows *which* car. It was a hit and run. Outrageous!"

"Weren't there any witnesses? Right in the middle of the day?"

"No," said Mr. Smith. "It was twelve noon exactly. Everyone was having lunch. They all heard the smash, but by the time they'd come out to have a look, the car had gone round the corner."

"And the fishmonger?"

"He doesn't know either. One moment he was gutting some herring, the next thing he's upside down, stall and all. The police have questioned everyone here in the neighborhood, but no one saw the car. It must have been a stranger, someone from out of town."

Tibble looked around. There was a cat eating something on the corner of the square. The cats must have seen who it was, he thought. And I bet Minou has already been informed.

He was right.

"We've known who it was for ages," she said when Tibble

arrived back upstairs. "Everyone's told everyone else up on the rooftops. It was Mr. Ellmore's car. He was in it too. It was him."

Tibble could hardly believe it. "Come on," he said. "Why would a man like that keep driving after an accident? He'd report it straightaway."

"The cats saw it," Minou said. "You know how there's always cats hanging around the fish stall. Cross-Eyed Simon was there, and so were the School Cat and Ecumenica. They all saw it. Now you can put it in the paper."

Tibble sat down and started chewing his fingernails.

"That's right, isn't it?" asked Minou. "This can go in the paper, can't it?"

"No," said Tibble. "I'll write an article about the accident. But I can't say Ellmore was the driver. There's no proof."

"No proof? But *three* cats—"

"Yes, *cats*! But what good's that? There wasn't a single witness."

"There were three witnesses."

"Cats aren't witnesses."

"No?"

"No. I can hardly write in the paper: 'According to information we have received from several cats, the vehicle that smashed into the fish stall was driven by prominent Killenthorn resident Mr. Ellmore.' I just can't. Don't you understand that?"

Minou didn't understand. She left the room and got into her box without a word.

* * *

At night on the roof Cross-Eyed Simon said, "There's someone waiting for you at the town hall."

"Who?"

"The Deodorant Cat. He's got news."

Minou went straight there. It was three in the morning and very quiet on the square. Two marble lions were crouched in front of the Town Hall, each with a marble shield between its knees.

Minou waited. A mixture of strange smells was wafting out from the left lion's shadow. She could smell cat *and* perfume. And now the Deodorant Cat emerged.

"Nosey-nosey first," he said.

Minou held out her nose.

"Sorry about the apple blossom," the cat said. "It's our latest fragrance. I've got something to tell you, but you mustn't tell anyone you got it from me. You have to keep my name out of the papers. Promise?"

"I promise," said Minou.

"Well . . . remember I told you about Billy? The boy who worked in our cafeteria and got fired?"

"Oh, yes," said Minou. "What about him?"

"He's back. He got his job back."

"He must be pleased," Minou said. "But is that all? It's not really newspaper material."

"Don't interrupt," said the Deodorant Cat. "I'm not finished. Listen. This afternoon I was sitting on the ledge. Outside on the wall there's a ledge, and when I sit on it, behind the creeper, I can hear and see everything that goes on in the owner's office. Our owner is Mr. Ellmore. Do you know who that is?"

"Of course I do!" Minou exclaimed. "He crippled your mother!"

"Exactly," said the cat. "That's why I hate him. Not that I see much of my mother these days. She smells a little too vulgar to my taste. I'm used to more refined fragrances. But that's not the point. I was sitting there on the ledge and I saw Billy in Ellmore's office and I thought, let's have a little listen, you never know."

"Go on," said Minou.

"I heard Ellmore say, 'That's agreed, then, Billy, you get your old job back. Just run along straight to the cafeteria.' And Billy said, 'With pleasure, sir, lovely, sir, thank you very much, sir.'"

"And that was the end of it?" asked Minou.

"I thought so at first," said the cat. "I thought it was over and I dozed off a little . . . because the sun was shining and you know what that's like . . . sitting on a ledge in the sun. . . ."

"Yes, I know," Minou said. "Go on."

"Well, all at once I heard Ellmore whispering something at the door: '. . . and don't forget . . . if anyone happens to ask you what you saw this afternoon on Green Square . . . you didn't see a thing. Understood? Not a thing.'

"'No, sir,' said Billy, 'Not a thing.' And he left the office. And that was that."

"*Aha*," said Minou. "I get it. Billy must have seen the accident."

"That's what I thought too," said the cat.

"Now we finally have a human who saw it," Minou told Tibble. "A real witness. Not just a cat witness."

"I'll go see Billy right now," said Tibble. "Maybe he'll admit to seeing something if I ask him straight out."

He left.

While Tibble was gone, Minou had a conversation on the roof with the cat from the hotel. The Metropole Cat.

"Tell me," Minou said. "I hear that Ellmore sometimes eats at the hotel. Is that true?"

"Yes," said the Metropole Cat. "He and his wife have dinner in our restaurant once a week. On Fridays. That's tonight."

"Could you sit close by?" Minou asked. "To listen in on what he says?"

"Not likely," said the Metropole Cat. "He kicked me once under the table."

"It's just that we'd really like to know what he's saying in private," Minou explained, "but none of us dare go to his house to eavesdrop. Because of his dog . . . Mars . . . So if you could, try to get close to the table."

"I'll see what I can do," the Metropole Cat promised.

Tibble came home much later, worn out and disheartened.

"I went to see Billy," he said. "But Billy says he didn't see anything. He insists he wasn't even in Green Square when it happened. I'm sure he's lying. He's too scared to say anything, of course. I went to see the fishmonger too, in the hospital."

"How is he?" Minou asked. "Did he still smell good?"

"He smelt like hospitals," Tibble said.

"How sad."

"I asked him, 'Could it have been Mr. Ellmore's car?' But

the fishmonger just got angry and shouted, 'What a stupid idea! Ellmore's my best customer, he wouldn't do something like that.' And . . ." Tibble hesitated. "I went to the police too. I asked them, 'Could it have possibly been Mr. Ellmore's car?'"

"And what did they say?" Minou asked.

"They burst out laughing. They thought I'd gone mad."

—11—

THE PUMP CAT AND
THE METROPOLE CAT

"Hasn't your human written about Ellmore in the paper yet?" the Tatter Cat asked.

"No," Minou said. "He says he doesn't have any proof."

"What a coward! How gutless can you get! Humans are the most useless animals around! They're as spineless as dogs," the Tatter Cat cried. She was so wound up, she forgot to keep an eye on her babies. One of the little tortoiseshell kittens had walked almost all the way to the camper door. When the mother cat saw it, she shouted, "Hey, look at that! Someone's ready for the great outdoors! Come here, you dope!" She grabbed the baby cat by the scruff of the neck and pulled it back to the blanket and the rest of the litter. "They're starting to be a real handful," she said. "The little whippersnappers."

The kittens had their eyes open. They kept tumbling over each other and playing with each other's tails. And with their mother's tattered, stringy tail.

"How's your leg?" Minou asked.

"It's a bit better. I'm still limping though. It's probably permanent. Every day I go out to drink from the puddle under the tap and it takes me ages to get there."

"Can you leave the children alone that long?" Minou asked anxiously. "Is it safe?"

"Nobody ever comes here," the Tatter Cat said. "Just you and Bibi. She brings me something every day too. And today she took photos of the little riffraff. Pictures of all those ugly little monsters! Weird, huh? Oh, yeah, before I forget . . . their father, the Pump Cat, asked if you could drop by on your way past. He's got something to tell you. Don't ask me what, but it's probably something to do with the fishmonger's accident."

Minou said goodbye and walked over to the gas station. The Pump Cat said a friendly hello.

"I don't know if it's worth bothering about," he said, "but I thought . . . it can't do any harm to mention it."

"Mention what?"

"Ellmore was here. He had a big dent in his bumper. And a smashed headlight."

"Ah!" said Minou.

"He's got two cars," the Pump Cat said. "It was the big one, the blue Chevy. You know we've got a garage here as well as a gas station. So he says to my human, the mechanic, 'I ran into my own garden wall. Could you fix it today?' And my human says, 'That's gonna be difficult.'"

"And then?" Minou asked.

"Then Ellmore gave him some money. I couldn't see how much, but it must have been a lot because my human looked very happy. And then Ellmore said, 'If anyone should ask any questions . . . about dents in my car or anything like that . . . I'd rather you didn't mention it.'"

"Aha," said Minou. "Thanks. I'll see you later."

While she was heading off, she turned and called back, "You've got some lovely kids there."

"Who?" asked the Pump Cat.

"You."

"Me? Who says so?"

"The Tatter Cat."

"She says all kinds of things," scoffed the Pump Cat.

The Metropole Cat was a gleaming, pitch-black tom with a white chest. He was also extremely fat from the luxurious life he led in the hotel dining room. At mealtimes, he wandered slowly from table to table, looking up at the hotel guests with pitiful, pleading eyes, as if to say, can't you see I'm starving to death? Most people gave him something, and gradually he'd grown fatter and fatter. He waddled.

It was Friday evening around six-thirty, and the dining room was fairly full. Waiters were walking in and out; knives and plates rattled; people were eating and chatting; it smelt of roast beef and roast potatoes.

Sitting in a corner by the window, a little to one side, were Mr. and Mrs. Ellmore.

The Metropole Cat made a tentative approach. He'd promised Minou to listen in, but because Ellmore had once kicked him under the table, he was being cautious. He sat down a few feet away and didn't go any closer. They were arguing, he could tell that from their gestures and faces, but unfortunately they were arguing under their breath.

I'm definitely not going to sit under the table, thought the cat. I'd get a boot straightaway. But if I go and sit next to *her* chair, I'll be safe enough.

Now he was close enough to hear what they were saying.

"So incredibly stupid of you," said Mrs. Ellmore. "You should have reported it immediately."

"You're not going to start all over again, are you?" said Mr. Ellmore. "Stop nagging."

"I still think you should have reported it," she persisted. "You still can."

He shook his head fiercely and stabbed a piece of meat with his fork.

The Metropole Cat took another step closer.

"Get lost, you nasty little monster," Mr. Ellmore hissed. But the cat stayed where it was and looked up at him with a very innocent and very hungry expression.

"Don't talk rubbish," Mr. Ellmore continued. "It's too late now. Of course you're right. . . . I *should* have reported it at once . . . but I didn't. And now it's too late."

"But what if it gets out?"

"It can't. Nobody saw it, except for a dim-witted ex–cafeteria assistant from the factory, and I gave him his job back right away."

"And the garage where you're getting the car fixed?"

"The mechanic will keep his mouth shut. He's a buddy of mine. Through thick and thin."

"I *still* think you should go and report it," Mrs. Ellmore said stubbornly.

"Will you just give it a rest? You think I'm mad? I've gone to so much trouble to get people here in town on my side. I've donated money left, right and center, one charity after the other. All to make people like me, all to get *in*. I've joined associations, I'm the president of this, that and the other, I'm on committees . . . I've done everything I can to make people trust me. And I've succeeded!"

The Metropole Cat took another sneaky step forward.

"Psst, scat!" hissed Mr. Ellmore. "That cat's enough to put you off your dinner!"

The black cat waddled off, did a small circuit of the dining room, and returned to the same spot. He heard Ellmore saying, "What if it got in the paper! My good name would be ruined. And then I wouldn't be voted onto the council committee. And the expansion of the factory wouldn't go ahead. I'd have everyone against me. And now let's change the subject. What are you having for dessert?"

"Cassata ice cream," said Mrs. Ellmore.

"And if I ever bump into that disgusting cat in the dark, I'll strangle it," her husband said, glaring at the fat black tom.

The Metropole Cat had heard enough. He strolled out through the door and dragged himself up to the rooftops to report back to Minou.

* * *

"Another *cat* who's overheard him," Tibble complained. "We still don't have a real witness. How can I write an article without proof? And the two people who could help me, Billy and the mechanic, refuse to speak up. They both claim they don't know anything about it."

"But you do believe the cats now, don't you?" Minou asked.

"Yes," said Tibble. "I believe you."

"I hope one day I'll get to give Ellmore a good scratch," said Minou.

"I hope so too," said Tibble.

It made him feel very despondent. He was convinced the cats were telling the truth, but he didn't dare write about it without any evidence. Besides being despondent, he was also angry. Angry and indignant. And all that anger made him less shy. It made him brave enough to approach people and ask them all kinds of questions.

But whenever he casually said, "I've heard that Mr. Ellmore caused that accident with the fish stall," people were outraged. "Where'd you get that idea? Who's spreading stories like that? Mr. Ellmore would *never* do anything of the kind! First of all, he's a careful driver, and second, he'd have owned up to it straightaway. He would *never* drive off like that. . . ."

"No, Tibble," Mr. Smith said. "You're talking complete and utter rubbish. That's nothing but cheap gossip."

—12—

THE TATTER CAT'S BABIES

Mrs. Van Dam said to her husband, "I used to have a small green teapot. Whatever did I do with it?"

"I haven't got a clue," said Mr. Van Dam. But a little later he said, "Didn't we used to keep that teapot in the camper? In our old camper."

"Oh, yes . . . that's right. Well, it's gone, then, with the camper, to the wreckers. Because that's what we did with that old camper, we took it to the wreckers!"

"Now that you mention it," said Mr. Van Dam, pondering the question, "I think it's still at the back of that parking lot. Remember?"

"After all these years?"

"It's been a while."

"I'll go have a look," said Mrs. Van Dam. "Maybe the teapot's still there. . . . It was such a handy little thing. There might be other things we can use too."

And so it was that Mrs. Van Dam walked into the parking lot just when the Tatter Cat had gone for a drink. Like every day, the Tatter Cat dragged her crippled leg along behind her on her way to the puddle under the tap. She'd always left her babies behind by themselves and nothing had ever happened; they'd never come to any harm because it was such an out-of-the-way spot where there were never any people.

But now Mrs. Van Dam pushed the door open and stepped inside.

The first thing she saw was the whole gang of kittens on the old blanket.

"Well, I never!" She scowled. "In my camper! A whole litter of kittens . . . and neglected, filthy kittens at that. And they're on *my* blanket."

It was a very old blanket. Torn and dirty. But Mrs. Van Dam still thought it was too good for the kittens. She grabbed an old floral pillowcase and dumped the six little kittens into it.

Then she picked up the green teapot and a tablecloth and a torn mat and said, "There."

She left with a bag in one hand and the pillowcase full of kittens in the other.

The Tatter Cat saw her leaving the caravan, but she was still a long way away. And she couldn't run. She limped home as fast as she could, dragged herself up the steps, and saw that her babies were gone. A mournful, howling caterwaul rang out over the parking lot, but no one heard it because the radio was playing in the gas station. And Mrs. Van Dam would have ignored it anyway, even if she had heard it. She stood next to the gas pump and looked down uncertainly at the heavy bag of kittens in her hand.

What on earth am I going to do with these cats? she thought. I can't take them home with me. What do I want with six dirty little kittens?

Now she saw that there was a car next to the pump. A big blue car. Mr. Ellmore was buying gas.

Mrs. Van Dam went over to him. She bent over and said, "Oh, hello, Mr. Ellmore," through the open side window.

"Hello, Mrs. Van Dam."

"I have a litter of kittens here. I found them in my old camper. I've got them in an old pillowcase. May I give them to you?"

"To me?" Mr. Ellmore asked. "What would I do with a litter of kittens?"

"Well," said Mrs. Van Dam, "I read that you're the president of the Animal Lovers' Association. You are, aren't you?"

"Yes, that's right," said Mr. Ellmore.

"Well, what that association is for . . . I mean . . . the aim of that association is to make sure the little creatures have a home. That's what I read."

"Yes, but right now I don't have much time," said Mr. Ellmore.

"And if there's no home available," Mrs. Van Dam continued, "you'd take them somewhere where they could be put down painlessly. It said that too. . . . So could you take care of that for me? I'll put them in the back."

She laid the bulging floral pillowcase on his backseat, gave him a friendly nod, and hurried off.

Leaving Mr. Ellmore sitting there with a bag of kittens in his car.

"The woman thinks I run a cat shelter," he growled. "What am I supposed to do with a bunch of kittens?"

He drove off.

The poor Tatter Cat stayed in the caravan moaning and mewling for a moment, and by the time she came out again, Mrs. Van Dam was gone. But the Pump Cat walked up to her.

"They've taken your kids," he said. "In a bag. In Ellmore's car. He drove off with them."

The Tatter Cat sat down and started whimpering.

She knew now that her little ones were lost, that there was no point in looking for them, that they might already be dead. And to make things worse, she could hardly move. She was totally helpless.

"I'll pass the news on," the Pump Cat said. "To the Cat Press Agency. I don't know if it will do any good."

The Tatter Cat couldn't speak. She whined softly.

"Well, good luck," said the Pump Cat. "It's a tough break."

As he walked off, the Tatter Cat called out after him, "They're your babies too."

The Pump Cat turned back for a moment. "That remains to be seen," he snarled.

The Cat Press Agency was always very fast. But no news had ever come through this fast. In less than ten minutes, Minou had heard it from Fluff.

"Where did Ellmore take them?" she asked quickly.

"His car's in front of the post office."

"Are the kittens still in it?"

"No," Fluff said, shaking his head sadly. "They're not there anymore. Simon looked in through the window. The car's empty."

"Where are they then?" Minou asked. "What's he done with them?"

"No one knows," Fluff said. "The Pump Cat saw him drive off and Ecumenica saw him drive past the church. And later a few cats spotted the car at the post office. But nobody saw what he did with the kittens."

"Maybe he drowned them somewhere," Minou cried. "Oh, this is terrible. The poor Tatter Cat. She was always calling them names, but she was so proud of her children. Let's get all the cats searching and tell them to keep their eyes and ears open. . . . I'll go out and start searching too."

She went down to the street and headed off in the direction of the post office. The cats she met on the way couldn't tell her any more than she'd already heard. Not a single cat had seen what had happened to the pillowcase. They'd only seen the car driving around and, later, parked and empty.

Minou didn't know where to look and wandered aimlessly through the back lanes until finally Muffin, the Bakery Cat, came running up to her.

"They've found them," she called. "The School Cat heard them squeaking!"

"Where?"

"In a rubbish bin near the post office. Hurry, we can't get them out."

Minou was there in less than a minute.

All six kittens were still alive. They were still in the floral pillowcase; they'd been dumped, pillowcase and all, in a big gray rubbish bin. The little tykes squeaked and trembled as Minou pulled them out one by one, but they were alive.

Just up the road the rubbish truck had started its round. . . . If Minou had arrived just a few minutes later, the bin containing the Tatter Cat's children would have been emptied into the back of the truck. They would have been crushed.

Carefully, she put the six kittens back into the pillowcase to take them with her. And she stroked the School Cat, who had found them. "That was brilliant," she said. "Thanks. Just in the nick of time . . ."

"I've got some news too," the School Cat said.

"Tell me. . . ."

"Henry the Eighth got divorced."

Minou didn't take the kittens back to the caravan. She took them to the attic and laid them in her own box for now.

"What's the idea?" said Fluff. "You're not planning on keeping them here, are you?"

"Absolutely," said Minou. "And the Tatter Cat too. I'm going to go get her now."

"I'm not sure I approve of that," said Fluff. But Minou had already climbed out through the kitchen window.

The Tatter Cat hadn't heard the news yet. She kept circling the camper, going in every now and then as if the babies might have reappeared inside in the meantime. And she kept meowing helplessly. No matter how rumpled and grimy the Tatter Cat had been . . . she'd never been *pathetic*. She'd always remained proud and cheerful. But not anymore. Now she was a sad little stray, miserable and inconsolable.

Until Minou suddenly appeared on the camper step.

"We've found them," she said. "All six. They're at our house. In the attic."

The Tatter Cat didn't show any signs of being happy. She just sat up a little straighter.

"Get them back here, then," she snapped.

"No," Minou said. "It's not safe here. You know that now. I've come to get you."

"Who? *Me*?"

"Yes, you."

"I don't let anybody *come and get* me," the Tatter Cat said with icy contempt. "Nobody *comes and gets* me."

"It's only temporary," Minou said. "In a few weeks we'll look for homes for your children. Until then, you're coming with me."

"Over my dead body."

"Your children still need you. They need to feed."

"Bring them here and I'll feed them."

There was no point in trying to argue with the Tatter Cat. And you couldn't take her anywhere against her wishes. She'd fight you tooth and claw.

But Minou was just as stubborn. "If you want them, come and get them," she said. "You know where I live."

The Tatter Cat shouted something at her as she left. It was the worst insult she knew: "Human!"

* * *

Minou made a soft nest for the kittens in the corner of the junk room. Tibble wasn't home, he was off wandering around town in search of evidence.

"I don't know that I'm really happy about this," Fluff complained. "I can't say I'm pleased. Six howling strangers in my attic . . . but yeah, just go ahead, make yourself at home."

"It's only temporary," Minou said.

"All we need now is for the mother to show up too," Fluff said. "You needn't think I'm going to put up with *that*."

Minou didn't reply. She stood at the kitchen window and looked out over the rooftops.

An hour later the Tatter Cat did show up. Slowly and with great difficulty, she'd climbed up to the rooftops with one lame leg. With her last bit of strength, she dragged herself through the gutter and let Minou lift her down through the window.

She didn't say anything. Minou didn't say anything either. She just put the Tatter Cat down next to her babies, who squealed with delight, squirmed, and began feeding at full speed.

"What did I say?" said Fluff. "The mother too. And now I know I'm not going to put up with it."

He fluffed up his tail, put back his ears and let out a horrific growling sound.

"Behave yourself, Fluff," Minou said. "And keep out of the junk room."

As long as the Tatter Cat stayed close to her children, everything went well, but as soon as she stepped away for even a moment, on her way to the kitchen or in search of the litter box . . . it was all-out war.

And just when Tibble came in, a furious fight was in full swing. A screeching tangle of fur rolling over and over on the floor with big tufts of hair flying everywhere.

"What's going on, for goodness' sake? Have we got *another* cat?" Tibble cried.

"We've got another *seven* cats," said Minou, pulling Fluff and the Tatter Cat apart.

She told him what had happened.

"You mean Ellmore dumped live kittens in a rubbish bin?" Tibble asked.

"That's exactly what I mean," said Minou. And now, finally, Tibble got really angry.

—13—

TIBBLE IS WRITING!

"Eight cats in the house," Tibble mumbled. "Nine, really . . . if I count Minou. Talk about crowded."

It was crowded. The kittens were already quite mobile. They crawled around everywhere, they climbed up on chairs, they scratched the couch and curtains, they sat on Tibble's paper and played with his pen. But he didn't mind. He even felt honored that the Tatter Cat was willing to live in his flat. He knew the old stray had never wanted to live with people ever . . . and now she was even sitting on his lap and letting him scratch behind her ears.

"You can stay here with us for the rest of your life," Tibble said.

"That's what you think!" the Tatter Cat cried, leaping off

his knee. "As soon as the brats are big enough, I'm back on the street."

Tibble didn't understand her. He was just glad that the fighting had stopped. The two big cats hissed and spat at each other now and then, and sometimes spent half an hour glaring and growling, but they kept themselves under control.

Suddenly Tibble said, "And now quiet, everyone. I've got some writing to do."

He sat down at his desk with a fierce look on his face.

Minou asked hesitantly, "Are you going to write an article?"

"Yes," said Tibble.

"Oh," said Minou. "Are you going to write *the* article? About Ellmore?"

"Yes," said Tibble. "And I couldn't care less if I don't have any proof. Witnesses leave me cold."

He tapped away on his typewriter. Now and then he disentangled a kitten from his hair and put it down on the floor. Now and then he slid two kittens off his sheet of paper. He kept typing away.

Fluff and the Tatter Cat forgot to feud. They sat watching him quietly and respectfully and the news passed from cat to cat over the roofs of the entire neighborhood. "Tibble is writing! Tibble is finally writing! Have you heard the news? It's going to be in the paper at last. . . . Tibble is writing!"

When Tibble had finished the article, he took it in to the paper.

In the newspaper building, he met the Editorial Cat. For the first time the cat looked up at him with respect and appreciation.

And after he had delivered his article and was crossing Green Square on the way home, he noticed a lot more cats than usual out on the street. They came up to him, brushed past his legs affectionately and called out, "Well done . . . finally!"

He didn't understand them, but he got the meaning.

Mr. Ellmore was sitting in the office of the editor of the *Killenthorn Courier*.

The morning newspaper was open on the desk and Ellmore was pointing at an article.

"What's the meaning of this?" he asked. He was pale, and his voice was trembling with anger.

Now it was the editor who was biting his nails nervously. "I'm afraid I didn't know anything about it," he said. "I've only just read it. . . . It got into the paper without my knowing."

"That doesn't make any difference!" Ellmore shouted. "This is slander. And it's *your* newspaper."

The Editorial Cat sat on the windowsill listening with big, shocked eyes and its ears up.

"I'm terribly sorry," the editor sighed. "The young man who wrote this is always extremely reliable. . . . He writes excellent articles. It's never just rumors, it's always the truth, and—"

"Are you claiming *this* is the truth?" Ellmore screamed.

"Oh, no, no, most definitely not . . ."

My editor is a coward too, thought the Editorial Cat.

"I just meant that I've never needed to read his articles beforehand. . . . They've always been correct. That's how this got in the paper without my knowing."

"I demand," said Ellmore, pounding the table with his fist, "I *demand* that this young man write a new article today setting this straight."

"An excellent solution," said the relieved editor. "I'll make sure of it."

The Editorial Cat had heard enough. He jumped down from the windowsill and hurried up to the roof to tell Minou.

"Listen . . . ," said the cat.

Minou listened.

"Thanks," she said.

And she went inside to tell Tibble.

"So," said Tibble. "Now I know what to expect."

The telephone rang. It was Tibble's boss.

"I have to go into work," Tibble told Minou a little later. "He wants to talk to me right away."

Nine pairs of cats' eyes watched him walk down the stairs.

"I'm making a very reasonable request, Tibble," said the editor. "You've made an enormous blunder. You've written something that has offended one of Killenthorn's best-known and most respected citizens. Your article's not just offensive, it's also *untrue*. Where on earth did you get such a ridiculous idea? That it was Mr. Ellmore who crashed into the fish stall!"

"It's true," said Tibble.

"What proof have you got? Where's the evidence? Who are your witnesses? Who saw it happen?"

"A few people know about it," Tibble said.

"Really. Who? And why haven't they said anything?"

"They're scared of Mr. Ellmore. He's got them under his thumb. They don't dare to speak up."

"Well," his boss sighed. "It all sounds extremely unlikely to me. But, as I said, you've got a chance to make up for it. All you have to do is write a nice article about Mr. Ellmore. Stating clearly, of course, that it was all your fault and a stupid mistake. And that you're sorry. And besides that, he asked if you could write something nice about the Deodorant Factory. How great it is to work in the factory. And about all the lovely fragrances you can get in a spray can. And how terrible it would be if we didn't have any deodorant . . . how much everyone would stink . . . Anyway, you get the idea. . . . And how essential it is that the factory be expanded. So you're going to do that today, Tibble. Agreed?"

"No," said Tibble.

It went quiet for a moment. The Editorial Cat was back up on the windowsill and winked at Tibble to encourage him.

"No? What do you mean, *no*? Are you refusing?"

"Yes, that's exactly what I'm doing," Tibble said.

"This is getting serious," the boss said. "You've been going so well recently. And now your pigheadedness is going to cost you your job. Be sensible, Tibble."

Tibble looked the Editorial Cat in the eyes.

"I'm sorry," he said. "But I'm not doing it."

"It's a shame," his boss sighed. "But you're not leaving me any choice. You're finished here, Tibble. You can go."

And Tibble left.

* * *

103

On the street he met Mr. Smith.

"What have you done now, Tibble?" he asked. "I just got the paper out of the letter box and what do I read? Gossip! Lies! Mr. Ellmore, the president of our Animal Lovers' Association . . . dumping kittens in a rubbish bin? And knocking down the fish stall . . . and not reporting it . . . and just driving off? Tibble, where do you get this nonsense? Bah! And I was going to ask you if you'd like to come to my reading. I'm holding a reading next week about 'The Cat Through the Ages.' I wanted to ask if you'd like to write an article about it. But now I'm not sure you're the right person for the job. . . ."

"I can't do it anymore anyway," Tibble said. "I'm no longer with the newspaper."

And he walked on with his head hanging.

"Now I've been fired after all, Miss Minou," he said. "First I was able to keep my job because of the cats; now I've lost it again because of the cats. But I'm not in the least bit sorry."

He sat down on the couch and the cats sat around him looking serious. Even the little ones could feel how serious things were—they hardly played with his shoelaces at all.

"We haven't given up yet," Minou said. "We've got something planned for tonight. As soon as it's dark, all the cats from the whole neighborhood will come to meet on our roof. We're going to have a Meowwwow."

That evening Tibble stayed home with the kittens, who were too little to go to a meeting. He could hear the Meowwow perfectly, though.

He couldn't guess how many cats there were, but, going by the sound, it must have been at least a hundred. They screeched, they squealed, and every now and then they sang the Yawl-Yowl Song.

At about eleven o'clock the doorbell rang.

It was Mrs. Van Dam. She came panting up the stairs in her fur coat and snapped, "Mr. Tibble, I've talked to my husband about it and we think enough's enough."

"What do you mean?" Tibble asked.

"This is no longer a respectable house, not with you living in it. It's become a hotbed of cat activity. Just listen. . . . Listen to them."

On the roof the caterwauling started up again.

"It's unbearable," Mrs. Van Dam continued. "And here . . . What's this I see? Six kittens as well. If I'm not mistaken they're the little beasts I found in my caravan. Six kittens plus those two big cats, plus that strange lady who's more cat than person . . . that's nine! Plus another hundred on the roof, that's a hundred and nine . . ."

"Plus twenty dead cats," said Tibble, "that's a hundred and twenty-nine."

"*What do you mean?*"

"I mean your coat. There's twenty in that."

This made Mrs. Van Dam absolutely furious. "The cheek of you," she yelled. "My mink coat! Are you claiming it's cat fur? Are you trying to insult me, like you insulted poor Mr. Ellmore in the newspaper? Because I read it! It's a disgrace. And that's why my husband and I agree that you have to go. Out of *my* attic. With all your kitties and caboodles. I'll give you until the end of the month. After which I shall rent my attic out to someone else. Good day, Mr. Tibble."

I shouldn't have said that about the fur coat, thought Tibble once she was gone. Not that it makes any difference. She would have kicked me out anyway. But it still wasn't very nice of me. And now I'm going to bed.

Tibble went to bed. He was so exhausted he slept right through the Meowwow and didn't even feel the six little kittens tickling and scratching his face. He didn't hear Fluff come home. And he didn't hear the Tatter Cat either, screeching for her children to come to her. And he didn't notice Minou getting into her box.

When he woke up it was eight o'clock in the morning. What was the horrible thing that had happened? he thought. Oh yeah, I lost my job. *And* I got kicked out of my flat. What do I do now? Where can I go with nine cats . . . and how am I supposed to bring home enough fish for such a large cat family? He wanted to talk to Minou about it, but she'd already gone out.

She was sitting in the park with Bibi.

"The cats of Killenthorn have a plan," she said. "And we wanted to ask you if you'd help us, Bibi."

"Sure," Bibi said. "How?"

"I'll tell you just what you need to do," Minou said. "Listen carefully."

—14—

FAR TOO MANY CATS

Mr. Ellmore was walking down the street. He had parked his big blue car, which was once again completely free of dents, and now he was on his way to the shoe shop to buy a pair of shoes.

For the first time he noticed how many cats there were in Killenthorn. He couldn't take a step without a cat getting in the way. Some of them even shot through between his legs. Twice he stumbled over a cat.

We really need to get rid of some of these cats, he thought. It's a cat plague, that's what it is. Next time I'll bring Mars with me.

And after a while he noticed that the cats were following him. First it was just one trailing along behind him, but when he looked again a little later there were eight of them.

And by the time he made it to the shop there were more than ten. They all followed him in.

"*Kssss!*" hissed Mr. Ellmore angrily. He chased them out of the shop, but they came back in again with the very next customer.

And when he was trying on shoes and standing there defenseless in his socks, they circled around him.

"Are these your cats, sir?" asked the shop assistant.

"What do you take me for?" Mr. Ellmore shouted. "They just followed me in."

"Shall I chase them away again?"

"Yes, please!"

The shop assistant chased the cats out for a second time, but as soon as the door opened again for a new customer, the whole horde came back in and crowded around Mr. Ellmore's legs.

He would have loved to kick them. He would have loved to catch one of them on the head with a heavy boot, but there were quite a few customers in the shop by now. And everyone knew him. Everyone knew he was the president of the Animal Lovers' Association. And that meant he wasn't allowed to kick any cats.

At least, not while people are looking, he thought grimly. But just wait. . . . I'll get my chance.

He got his chance. On the street all the cats trooped along behind him. As long as people were watching, he didn't dare do a thing, but when the street was quiet for a moment close to the school, he looked around quickly, saw that the coast was clear, and gave the Butcher's Cat a good kick.

The cats shot off in all directions.

"That's that taken care of," smirked Mr. Ellmore. But when he got to his car and opened the door he found eight or so cats sitting inside it. He was so furious he was about to bash them right out again when a voice behind him said, "Oh, look . . . how lovely."

He turned around and saw Mr. Smith beaming at him.

"A car full of cats," he said. "You're such an animal lover."

"Absolutely . . . ," said Mr. Ellmore with a strained smile.

"You *are* coming to my reading tomorrow, aren't you?" Mr. Smith asked. "I think *you* will find it particularly interesting: 'The Cat Through the Ages: A Feline History.' With beautiful colored slides. You'll be there, won't you?"

"Yes, definitely," said Mr. Ellmore.

The cats emerged sedately from the car. Mr. Ellmore drove to his factory. He had an important meeting in his office with the councillor. To discuss expanding his factory. But because of all the cats, he was late. When he walked into his office the councillor was already there.

Mr. Ellmore apologized, offered the councillor a cigar, and started talking about his expansion plans.

"There are a lot of people who aren't so keen on an expansion," the councillor said. "They're afraid the town will get too smelly."

"Oh, but our fragrances are wonderful," Mr. Ellmore said. "Our latest is apple blossom. . . . I'll just let you smell it."

But when he turned around to get the spray can, he saw three cats slipping out through the open window.

He suppressed a curse.

"Just smell how wonderful it is," he said.

The councillor sniffed.

"Apple blossom," said Mr. Ellmore. He sniffed too. But what they smelt wasn't apple blossom at all. The whole room reeked of tomcats.

"Cat pee," the councillor wanted to say. But he was a well-mannered man and said politely, "Mmmm, that smells good."

That afternoon Mr. Ellmore took his dog in the car with him, in case a troop of cats tried to follow him again.

And there they were. Standing around the parking spot. Some were close by, others at a distance. The whole street was crawling with cats.

Mr. Ellmore held the door open and said, "Come on out, Mars. Look, Mars . . . kitty-cats . . . come on, boy, get 'em!"

But to his surprise, Mars stayed in the car, quietly whimpering. He didn't want to get out.

"What are you doing? You're not scared of a few cats, are you?"

But Mars didn't stir. He growled viciously, but he was too scared to get out of the car.

He could see the Tatter Cat. She was the closest of all, and although she had a limp now and couldn't move that quickly, she was the bravest of all as well. She looked so mean, so devilish, with such a bloodthirsty expression on her dirty cat face. . . .

Mars suddenly remembered how she'd clawed him in his own backyard. And now there were all those other cats too. There were too many—he couldn't take them on. He was staying in the car.

"Call yourself a dog!" Mr. Ellmore said contemptuously.

He looked around. Lots and lots of cats ... not very many people ... and no one watching.

He grabbed the dog leash from the back of the car and lashed out left and right. He caught the Church Cat Ecumenica, who shot screeching into the church; the others disappeared in all directions, like a swarm of hornets when you spray them with water.

But just like hornets, they came back. The Tatter Cat leading the way. And they trailed along behind Mr. Ellmore until he drove off again.

That evening they went to his garden as well.

Until now Mars had always kept all the cats away. None of them had ever dared go into the garden, except now and then when the dog was shut in the garage. Like the time that led to the Tatter Cat's lame leg.

And now all of a sudden ... cats in the garden.

"Mars ... kitty-cats!" Mr. Ellmore called. "Get 'em, boy. Go on, get 'em!"

Mars jumped around excitedly in front of the french doors, but didn't dare go out into the garden.

"I don't understand what's got into the dog," Mr. Ellmore said. "He's scared of cats! Have you ever heard anything so ridiculous? A German shepherd that's scared of cats!"

"If I'm not mistaken, they're attacking our rosebushes," his wife said. "Chase them away! Here, take this bottle. Last time you hit that filthy stray with it."

Mr. Ellmore ran out with the bottle.

The cats were hard at work scratching the flowers and leaves off the roses Ellmore was so proud of.

They looked up at him triumphantly as he approached.

"Dirty rotten cats! Now there's nobody around to watch! Now I'm in my own garden. . . . I'll get you. . . ."

He lashed out left and right but stamped on his own roses in the process and stabbed himself with a thorn. And the cats were gone, disappearing between the bushes and trees.

"And you know what you'll get if I see you here again!" Ellmore roared at the bushes.

He went back inside and his wife said, "They're back."

"Where?"

"In the rose bed. They're going to destroy all our roses."

"That's it," her husband said grimly. "This is too much. And fortunately there aren't any people around here, so I don't have to restrain myself. Get me my hunting rifle!"

She fetched it for him.

He stood next to the terrace with the gun in his hands. Although it was already evening, the spring sun was shining down through the branches of the trees onto the rose bed, where no fewer than ten cats were ripping up the rosebushes with delight in their eyes.

"Now I'll get you . . . you scum . . . ," Mr. Ellmore said softly.

He raised the gun up to his shoulder.

Simon the Siamese was the closest. He looked at Ellmore with his eyes completely crossed but didn't budge.

Seven cats ran off in fright; three stood their ground. The Councillor's Cat, the Tatter Cat, and Cross-Eyed Simon.

Seconds before the shot rang out, they sped off—just in time. Only the Tatter Cat was still limping on the lawn, but before Mr. Ellmore could take aim again, she ducked into the shadows.

He turned around to go back inside but saw a girl standing there. A little girl in his garden. She tried to slip away, but he saw that she was laughing. She was laughing at him.

"What's the idea? What are you doing here?" Mr. Ellmore cried.

She was laughing so hard she couldn't answer.

Mr. Ellmore was beside himself with rage. He grabbed the girl by the arm and shook her hard.

"Now get out of my garden, you little brat."

At first it looked like Bibi was crying. But as soon as she was through the gate, she started laughing again.

She waited for a moment on the other side of the fence, on the street. Then Minou came out of the garden through a hole in the hedge. And behind her came the Tatter Cat . . . and all the other cats, one by one.

The rest of the evening they left the roses alone.

—15—

THE CAT
THROUGH THE AGES

"The reading's on tonight," Minou said. "Mr. Smith's talk. In the Metropole Hotel."

"I know," Tibble said. "I don't need to go anymore."

"They'll be showing slides," Minou said. "Of all kinds of special cats. In color."

"Maybe," Tibble said. "But I'm not going. I don't need to write any more articles. I don't work for the newspaper anymore. And anyway, I've got enough cats right here. Thanks, but no thanks."

"Everyone's going to be there," Minou said.

"Exactly," said Tibble. "And that's why I'd rather not go. Mr. Ellmore will be there too, of course, as the president of the association. And if I never see him again it will be too soon."

"I'm going," Minou said.

He looked up with surprise—Minou, who was so shy and so scared of going anywhere crowded.

"And I would like it very much if you could come with me," she said.

And now there was something about her voice that made him realize something special was going on. He couldn't imagine *what*, but after a slight hesitation he said, "All right, then."

Outside there was a poster saying:

ANIMAL LOVERS' ASSOCIATION
TONIGHT: *THE CAT THROUGH THE AGES: A FELINE HISTORY.*
A READING WITH SLIDES BY MR. W. SMITH

Tibble and Minou were the last to arrive. The hall was packed because Mr. Smith was extremely popular and a gripping speaker. And of course, the people of Killenthorn were crazy about cats.

Sitting in the front row was Mr. Ellmore, who was going to say a few words of welcome.

As it hadn't started yet, people were chatting among themselves, and when Tibble and Minou began looking for somewhere to sit, people around them whispered and pointed.

Two elderly ladies just behind them spoke softly to each other.

"That's the young man from the newspaper, you know. With his secretary."

"He's not with the paper anymore, though."

"No?"

"No, he wrote that outrageous article about Mr. Ellmore!"

"Was that him?"

"Absolutely, his name was at the bottom. And it said that our own Mr. Ellmore had run into the fish stall."

"Yes, and it also said that he'd dumped live kittens in a rubbish bin. Disgraceful things to write. Without a shred of evidence."

Tibble could hear every word. He felt more and more miserable and wished he'd stayed home. Next to him sat Minou, who was in an extremely catlike and inscrutable mood. And very calm . . . She seemed completely oblivious to everyone around her.

A little bit closer to the front sat Bibi, next to her mother.

Now Mr. Ellmore rose to speak a few words of welcome. He was met with enthusiastic applause.

While clapping, people kept sneaking backward looks at Tibble. It was as if they were trying to say: Even if you write nasty gossip, we don't believe you. We trust our Mr. Ellmore.

Mr. Ellmore gave a friendly smile and nodded. He kept it very short and handed the microphone over to Mr. Smith.

It was a fascinating reading. Mr. Smith spoke about cats among the ancient Egyptians. He spoke about cats in the Dark Ages and he showed slides.

The lights in the auditorium were off, and every time he tapped on the floor with his stick a new cat appeared on the screen.

"We will now have a fifteen-minute break," Mr. Smith said

116

after he had been talking for an hour. "In that time refreshments will be available at the buffet. But before we stop, I'll just show you *one* more slide of a most extraordinary pedigreed cat from the Renaissance."

He gave a tap with his stick. That was the sign that the boy operating the slide projector should show the last slide before the intermission.

A cat did appear on the screen. But it wasn't a pedigreed cat at all. It was a slide of the Butcher's Cat fetching a good kick on Green Square. And the person giving him the kick was Mr. Ellmore, who was clearly visible. It was true that the photo wasn't beautiful and it was very wonky, but there was no mistaking its content.

Tibble sat up straight. He looked at Minou. She smiled.

"That's *my* cat!" shouted the butcher from the second row. Mr. Smith tapped angrily with his stick and cried, "That is not the correct photo."

People started mumbling in the auditorium. And now the next slide appeared. This one showed Mr. Ellmore hitting the Church Cat Ecumenica with a dog whip. He was enjoying it very much, you could see that clearly.

"That's *our* cat!" cried the vicar, but the next slide had already popped up. And now Mr. Ellmore was standing next to the terrace in his own garden holding a gun. He was aiming at three cats.

"That's *my* Simon!" Mr. Smith cried indignantly.

"Our cat . . . ," whispered the councillor's wife.

The Tatter Cat was in the photo too, but no one worried about that except Tibble, who looked at Minou in dismay. She

117

gave him another friendly nod, and suddenly he understood the cats' plan. He realized that Bibi had taken the photos on the street and in Ellmore's garden with her new camera. Only Bibi could take photos *that* crooked.

The mumbling and whispering in the auditorium grew louder.

Everyone looked at Mr. Ellmore. It was fairly dark, but everyone could see that he'd stood up and walked to the front.

"It's not true," he shouted. "That's not me!"

But now the next slide appeared. Even more crooked than the others, but just as clear. Mr. Ellmore holding a girl by her arm and shaking her. The girl was Bibi.

"That's a fake!" Mr. Ellmore shouted. "I can explain everything. It's a trick!"

But by now the audience was talking so loudly that nobody heard him.

He walked to the back of the auditorium and the slide projector.

The boy who was showing the slides was Billy, the canteen assistant.

"Stop it at once!" Mr. Ellmore shouted.

"That was the last one," said Billy.

"You—" Ellmore said furiously. "You—where did you get those photos?"

"I'm just working through all of them," Billy said, "like I'm supposed to."

"But how did those last ones get in there?"

"How should I know?" asked Billy.

There was now an enormous uproar in the hall. Mr. Smith

tried to calm things down. "Ladies and gentlemen, this is all based on a regrettable misunderstanding," he said. "I suggest we all just have a quiet cup of coffee, after which I will resume my talk."

"You're fired!" Mr. Ellmore hissed quickly at Billy.

He went back into the middle of the hall, where the lights were back on and people were standing around in groups, talking as they pushed up to the buffet. Wherever Mr. Ellmore went, they suddenly fell quiet.

He'd wanted to explain, but there was nothing to explain. The photos had been all too clear. Mr. Ellmore shrugged helplessly and left.

No sooner had he left than the conversation picked up again on all sides.

"Unbelievable," said the councillor's wife. "The president of the Animal Lovers' Association. Shooting at cats! He shot at *my* cat!"

"He grabbed *my* daughter," said Bibi's mother. "That's much more serious. And to think that he's head of the Child Welfare Commission."

Bibi was sitting there very sweetly, as if none of it had anything to do with her.

"Why didn't you tell me?" her mother asked. "About that man grabbing you?"

But Bibi kept quiet. She looked at Tibble over her Coke bottle and whispered, "Good, huh?"

"Fantastic," he said.

"Minou took that one of me," she said. "She was in a tree." Tibble looked around to see if he could see Minou. He'd been

119

separated from her in the crowd. He walked around and heard scraps of conversations everywhere.

The two elderly ladies were talking again.

"It's quite possible that it was true after all, at least partly."

"What?"

"That article in the paper. About Ellmore dumping kittens in a rubbish bin."

"Yes, of course, a man like that is capable of anything. And that bit about the fish stall is sure to be true too."

Nearby, Mr. Smith was talking to Billy.

"How on earth did that happen, Billy?" Mr. Smith asked. "Those photos at the end . . . that wasn't the idea at all. How did they get in there?"

"Miss Minou gave them to me," said Billy. "She asked if I could show them before the break. I didn't know why, but she was *so* friendly. And she was *so* sweet when she asked me."

"I see . . . ," said Mr. Smith. "Well, well . . ."

"And now I've lost my job anyway," Billy went on, "so I can tell everyone too."

"Tell everyone what?" Mr. Smith asked.

"That I was there," said Billy.

"Where?"

"In Green Square. When Mr. Ellmore crashed into the fish stall."

"But, my boy!" Mr. Smith exclaimed. "Why didn't you say so before?"

Someone else came over to join them. The mechanic from the garage. "Then I might as well tell you what I know too," he said. "Mr. Ellmore's car was badly damaged."

"You shouldn't be telling *me* that," Mr. Smith said. "You have to tell the police. And there just happens to be a policeman here in the hall right now."

He went over to Tibble, who was still walking around by himself.

"Tibble," said Mr. Smith. "I'm afraid I misjudged you. I'm sorry. I believe you were right all along. You should write an article about this evening now."

"I'm no longer with the newspaper," said Tibble.

Minou, too, was walking around among all the people who were talking away and drinking their coffees. Now and then she caught snippets of conversation: "That Tibble fellow was telling the truth after all. . . . His article wasn't just gossip."

"You really think so?"

"I'm sure of it!"

And she felt very contented. This was just what the cats had hoped for when they made their plan.

She was about to return to her seat when she saw something black behind a glass door. It meowed.

Minou pushed open the door and stepped out into the hotel lobby.

The black shape was the Metropole Cat.

"I've been standing here calling you for hours," he moaned. "I was too scared to go in with all those people there. It went well, didn't it?"

"It went exceptionally well," Minou said. "Thanks to all the cats."

"Excellent," said the Metropole Cat. "But I called you because there's someone waiting for you outside."

"Who?" Minou asked.

"Your sister. Outside the revolving doors, in the shadow of the linden tree. If you have a moment."

Minou felt warm and cold all at once. Just like in Aunt Sooty's garden . . . Thinking about her sister made her throat throb strangely.

"I can't," she said. "I have to get back. There's a reading."

"Come off it," said the Metropole Cat. "What's that reading to you? What do you care about 'The Cat Through the Ages' when today's cat is out there waiting for you?"

"I'm not going," Minou said.

"Why not? You're not scared of your own sister, are you?"

"No . . . or . . . maybe," Minou said. "Tell her I can't come right now."

And when Tibble made it back to his seat, Minou was already there, on the chair next to his.

Mr. Smith finished his talk without any more unusual developments.

—16—

THE EDITORIAL CAT

The next morning there was a constant stream of cats up on the rooftops.

They'd all been informed. The cats had passed the word on from one to the other that very night.

"This is the best news since Dunkirk," said the School Cat.

They were sitting on the roof of the Social Security Building. Minou had never been in the middle of such a large group of cats before, and definitely not in broad daylight. She'd brought a bag of meat with her and was sharing it out on all sides. Ecumenica was so wild with joy that she burst into a fit of harsh screeching—quite unseemly for a Church Cat. "We're going to celebrate!" she screamed.

"Yeah, let's celebrate," the Tatter Cat said. She was proud

that she could climb up to the highest rooftop again despite her leg.

"There's nothing to celebrate," Minou said. "My human is still fired, and in a few days he'll have to move out of his flat."

"Wait and see," said Cross-Eyed Simon. "Anything could happen today. The mood's changed. People don't like Ellmore anymore. *My* human's furious with him."

"*Mine* too," said the councillor's cat.

"The whole town's talking about it," said the Metropole Cat. "And this time, I mean the people."

Meanwhile Tibble was stuck in the attic with the six little kittens. His big cats were out on the roof, including Minou.

He'd hardly seen her since the reading, and there were all kinds of things he was dying to ask her.

He wandered around the flat and didn't really know what to do with himself. Then the doorbell rang.

It was Mr. Van Dam, his downstairs neighbor. When he finally made it to the top of the stairs, he seemed a little bashful and didn't want to sit down.

"This won't take long," he said. "I've heard that my wife has given you notice to leave. That she wants you out of our attic. She did that without telling me. And she shouldn't have. I don't agree with it."

Tibble said, "Please, have a seat."

Mr. Van Dam sat down on the edge of a chair.

"Sometimes she overdoes things," he said. "She was angry because there were so many cats on the roof. But I told her right away, 'Tibble can't help that. That's just what this neighborhood's like. There happen to be a lot of cats around here.'"

Tibble nodded.

"And you having cats yourself," Mr. Van Dam continued, "that's not a problem for us at all. She says it is . . . but I disagree."

"Thank you," said Tibble.

"And otherwise she was very angry about that article of yours in the paper," Mr. Van Dam said. "But now we all know that you were absolutely right. It was true. I just heard that it was Ellmore who ran into the fish stall. And the police have finally found a couple of witnesses."

"Oh," said Tibble. "Great. I can't offer you a cigarette because I don't smoke, but would you like a peppermint?"

"I'd love one," said Mr. Van Dam. "You also had a . . . um . . . a secretary . . . somewhere." He looked around vaguely.

"Yes," said Tibble, "but she's not here right now. She's out on the roof."

"Cute little kittens," said Mr. Van Dam. "I'd love to have one."

"Oh," said Tibble, "you can. When they're a little bigger."

"No, I can't. My wife doesn't like cats, you see. There's no way round that. But there's *one* thing I want to tell you, Tibble: this is your home, and you can rent it from us as long as you like. That's all there is to it."

"That's fantastic . . . ," Tibble sighed.

He would have loved to tell Minou straightaway, but she wasn't there. And right after Mr. Van Dam went downstairs again, the phone rang.

It was Tibble's boss.

Asking if he could drop by shortly.

Half an hour later he was back in that old familiar spot, sitting in front of his boss's desk. And the Editorial Cat was there too and winked at him.

"By the looks of things, you were right, Tibble," the editor said. "That article you wrote was *true*."

"Of course it was true," Tibble said. "Otherwise I wouldn't have written it."

"Not so fast . . . ," his boss said. "That doesn't alter the fact that you didn't have the slightest bit of evidence. And you mustn't ever write something without evidence to back it up. What you did was wrong. Let's hope you never do it again."

Tibble looked up. "Again?" he asked.

"Yes. Because I hope you're willing to carry on here with us at the paper. You are, aren't you?"

"Oh, yes," said Tibble. "I'd love to!"

"Good, that's agreed, then. And . . . oh, yeah, Tibble . . . one last thing before you go: it's been a long time since you wrote anything about cats. It's all right if you want to write about them again sometimes. As long as it's not too often."

"Great," said Tibble.

As soon as the conversation was over, the Editorial Cat slipped out of the window and hurried up to the roof to tell Minou the news.

"Your human's back with the newspaper!"

Minou sighed with relief.

"So now you can go away again," the cat said.

"Go away? Where?"

"Well," said the Editorial Cat. "Your sister wants you back, doesn't she? You're allowed to go back to your old house now, aren't you?"

"I don't know . . . ," Minou said, very flustered all of a sudden. "Where did you hear that?"

"On the way here . . . from a couple of different cats. Haven't you spoken to her yet?"

"No," said Minou.

"You'll see her soon, then. She's coming to get you."

"But I don't want to move," Minou said. "I've already got a human. And he still needs me. How else is he going to get news?"

"He doesn't need you anymore," the Editorial Cat said. "He's changed so much! He's not shy anymore, not at all. He's not scared of anything. Haven't you noticed?"

"Yes," Minou said. "It's true. He's brave enough to go up to anyone and ask anything now. He was so angry at Ellmore, he stopped being scared. He Learnt to Dare."

On their way back to the attic, Minou talked a little with the Tatter Cat, who immediately brought up the subject of her sister.

"Your sister wants you to drop by," the Tatter Cat said. "I haven't spoken to her myself, but that's the message going round. I'd get over there if I were you."

"Yes . . ." Minou hesitated.

"I hear she's found some remedy that will cure you. That would be a real blessing," the Tatter Cat said. "The *bliss* of being a cat again . . . don't you think?" She peered at Minou with her yellow eyes.

"I . . . um . . . I don't know anymore . . . ," Minou said.

She found Tibble in the living room, over the moon about all the things that had been happening.

"I've got my job back, and my flat!" he shouted. "We're going to celebrate with fish, fried fish, and lots of it." But because he was so happy, he didn't notice how quiet Minou was. Quiet and thoughtful and not happy at all.

—17—

A CAT AGAIN?

Tibble was woken by a downy paw stroking his face.

It was Fluff.

Tibble looked at his alarm clock. "Quarter past three . . .
Fluff, why are you waking me up in the middle of the night?
Go back to the end of the bed and lie down."

But Fluff meowed insistently.

"Have you got something to say? Are you trying to tell me
something? You know I don't understand you. Go and tell
Minou. She should be in her box."

But Fluff kept meowing until Tibble got up.

Minou wasn't in her box. Apparently she was still out on
the roof. It was already starting to get light. The kittens were
playing in the junk room and Fluff kept meowing at Tibble
until he followed him over to the kitchen window.

"What is it? Do I have to look out?"

Tibble leant out of the window and looked out over the rooftops. There were two cats sitting nearby on the slanting roof. One was the Tatter Cat. The other was a beautiful ginger cat with a white chest and a white-tipped tail.

Tibble leant out farther and the window squeaked. The ginger cat looked at him.

He was so shocked he almost lost his balance and had to grab hold of the window frame. It was Minou.

The eyes he knew so well. Minou's eyes. And Minou's face, totally, but now *all* cat.

He wanted to call out, *Minou!* but the shock had made him hoarse and taken his breath away. It only lasted a moment anyway. The ginger cat turned and disappeared over the edge of the roof with a few quick jumps.

The Tatter Cat stayed where she was. She just flicked her tail and looked at him with her mysterious yellow eyes.

Feeling a little dizzy, Tibble went inside, sat down on the couch, and started to chew his nails.

"Ridiculous," he said. "Nonsense. I'm letting my imagination run away with me. Miss Minou will come back any moment now."

Fluff kept circling around him and trying to tell him something. Never before had Tibble *so* wished he understood Cattish. . . . *Something* was going on. . . . That was all he knew.

"What are you trying to tell me, Fluff? Has she changed back to a cat?"

"Ah, nonsense," he said again. "I'm still half asleep. I'm dreaming. I'm going back to bed."

He tried to go back to sleep but couldn't. He just lay there waiting. . . . Usually Minou came home as soon as it got light. Then she'd get in her box. Now she didn't come, and he grew more and more worried. In the end he got up to make some coffee.

It was six o'clock. And Minou still hadn't come home.

Tibble went to see if her things were still there.

Her washcloth and toothbrush and things. They were all there. Her case was still in the junk room too. That was a relief.

A relief? Why should it be a relief? Tibble thought. If she's changed back to a cat, she won't need any of that anymore.

I'm going mad. What kind of rubbish have I gotten into my skull?

At quarter past six the doorbell rang.

It's her! thought Tibble. She's coming up through the front door.

But it wasn't Minou. It was Bibi who came up the stairs.

"I know it's really early, Tibble," she said. "But I got such a fright. I looked out of my window this morning . . . I have a view out over the rooftops too, just like you . . . and I saw Minou. She went past."

"Yes?" said Tibble. "And?"

Bibi was silent for a moment and looked distraught.

"Go on, Bibi. . . ."

"She's turned back into a cat again," Bibi said. She said it hesitantly. She was afraid that Tibble would laugh at her. But Tibble stayed serious. He did say, "Bibi, come on . . . don't be silly. . . ." But he said it without any conviction.

"It's really true," Bibi said.

"I think I saw her too," Tibble said. "I went to call her, but she ran off. She could be anywhere now."

"I think she's gone back to her old house," Bibi said. "To her garden."

"Which garden?"

"On Victoria Avenue. She told me once that her real home was in Victoria Avenue. A house with a golden chain tree next to the patio. That's where she lived when she was still a cat."

Fluff started meowing again.

"I don't understand what he's saying," Bibi said. "But he's probably agreeing with us. What should we do, Tibble?"

"Nothing," Tibble said. "What can we do?"

"Go there," Bibi said. "To Victoria Avenue. To see if she's there."

"No," said Tibble. "That's ridiculous."

But ten minutes later they were walking down the street together in the early-morning light.

It was a very long way, and it took them a while to find Victoria Avenue. It was a short, winding street with white houses and big front gardens.

"I can't see a ginger cat anywhere," said Tibble. "I don't see a golden chain tree anywhere either."

"It must be at the back," Bibi said. "I'll go round and walk through the gardens. Nobody will be up this early."

It was very quiet on the street at this hour. Birds were singing and the blossoms were swaying in the breeze. Tibble sat down on a garden wall to wait for Bibi to come back. In front of one of the houses there was a big rubbish bin. The house itself wasn't being used as a home anymore; it looked more like offices. A sign on the gate said *Institute for Biochemical Research* in black letters.

And that reminded Tibble of something Minou had told him: that as a cat she'd eaten something from a rubbish bin that had changed her. He'd laughed about it at the time, but now he thought, who knows . . . with all these modern scientific experiments . . . They must have thrown out something that went wrong.

Bibi had reappeared next to him.

"It must be that one," she said, pointing at the house next door to the institute.

"There's a golden chain tree out the back. But I didn't see any cats. Maybe she's gone inside. *Oh, look!*"

Tibble looked.

The ginger cat was standing in the front garden. Under a lilac bush.

She turned her head to look at Tibble and Bibi, staring straight at them. And again they both saw Minou's eyes.

But the most horrific thing of all was that the cat had a thrush in her jaws. A freshly caught, live, fluttering thrush.

Bibi yelled and waved her arms and in a flash the cat ran off through the bushes at the side of the house with the bird in her mouth.

"I'm going after her!" Bibi cried, but Tibble stopped her.

"Don't," he said. "That bird's probably wounded and half dead . . . it's best to just leave it."

They stood there at the hedge. Minou had disappeared round the back of the house with her prey and Bibi started to cry.

"Don't cry," Tibble said. "It's just the way things are. You can't stop a cat from being a cat. And cats catch birds."

"I saw that expression on Minou's face a lot," said Bibi. "When we were in the park and a bird landed near us. I thought it was creepy. I'd shout out, 'It's not allowed.' And then she was always so ashamed of herself. But now she's not ashamed anymore. And that's why I'm crying."

Tibble was only half listening. He was wondering whether he should ring the doorbell. He wanted to ask, excuse me, ma'am, but was your ginger cat missing for a while?

But he thought about it and realized that the lady who lived here wouldn't even be up yet. It was still so early. And anyway . . . what difference did it make? She'd probably say, yes, she was gone for quite a long time, but now she's back.

What good would that do him?

"Come on, let's go," he said.

"Don't you want to take her with you?" Bibi asked.

"No," said Tibble. "She's someone else's cat. And I've still got eight cats left."

Slowly and silently they walked back through the streets.

It hadn't been a pleasant sight . . . their own Minou with a live bird between her jaws.

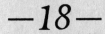

—18—

THE GINGER SISTER

It was still nighttime and pitch-black when Minou met her sister on the roof of the Social Security Building.

The Bakery Cat had come to tell her, "Your sister's waiting for you. It's urgent. You have to come at once."

Even before Minou saw her sister, she smelt the family smell. A very distinctive and very familiar smell of Home . . . and that was why she immediately said, "A quick nosey-nosey?"

"What do you take me for?" Her sister scowled. "Not until you're a proper cat again."

"I don't know if that's ever going to happen."

"Don't worry about that. It will. Tonight. The opportunity is *there*."

"Where?" Minou asked.

"I mean it's possible *now*. It wasn't possible before. And later it won't be either. This is your last chance. So come with me."

"You mean to your house?"

"I mean to *our* house. To *our* garden."

The enormous sky over the roofs seemed to be growing a little lighter in the east. Minou could now make out all of her sister's body. It didn't make her look any friendlier.

"You chased me away," Minou said. "You said you never wanted to see me again. You were angry about me taking the Woman's case and clothes. Even though I really couldn't leave without anything."

"Forgive and forget," her sister said quickly. "The Woman didn't even notice. She's got so many cases and so many clothes . . . you know that."

"But you were most furious about me not being a cat any more. You chased me out of the garden with your claws!"

"That was *then*," her sister said. "Tonight you can recover. Tonight or early tomorrow morning at the latest."

"How can you be so sure?"

"Perhaps you've heard," her sister said, "that I *almost* had the same thing?"

"Yes, Aunt Sooty told me."

"It wasn't as bad as with you. But I'd eaten out of that rubbish bin as well. And terrible things started happening. My whiskers disappeared and my tail grew smaller and smaller. And I got some very strange urges. I wanted to start walking on my hind legs. And I wanted to have a shower. Instead of washing myself properly with spit."

"And then?" Minou asked.

"A dusk thrush cured me," her sister said. "I ate a dusk thrush, that's all. You know how rare they are in our gardens. You hardly ever see them. They only pass through. But I just happened to catch one. And that reversed it. It cured me. . . . I know that dusk thrushes eat certain herbs that are good for all kinds of diseases. Yours too."

"And? Are they there now?" asked Minou.

"Only tonight. And maybe very early in the morning. That's why you have to come with me right away. It's already starting to get light."

Minou stayed sitting there and thought about it.

"Come on," said her sister. "Come home."

"But I've got a home," Minou said. "A home and a Man . . ." She fell silent. The attic and the Man seemed so terribly far away. And so unimportant. Her sister smelt so warm and so *close*.

"Remember how we used to catch starlings together in the garden?" her sister asked. "And how fabulous our garden is in spring? Think of the golden chain tree . . . it's in flower now. . . . Soon, when you've got your tail back, you can walk under the golden chain tree. You can sit on the Woman's lap and purr. You'll be able to do everything that's cattish and normal. What is there to think about? You're shivering, you're cold. Come with me, and soon you'll have your coat back."

Minou *was* cold. It would be lovely to have fur again, she thought. To stretch out on the paving stones in the sun in thick ginger fur. The bliss of licking yourself with one paw up in the air . . . and then gnawing between your toes. The pure bliss of having claws you can retract or put out, whichever you choose.

And spending ages scratching and scratching away at the leg of a brand-new chair.

"I'm coming," Minou said. "Just wait a moment. . . ."

"No, I'm not waiting . . . it's almost dawn. What else do you need?"

"I just wanted . . . I thought . . . I have to get my case . . . and my washcloth and that . . ."

"What?" her sister cried. "What do you need all that for? What good's a case to a cat?"

"I thought . . . maybe I could return it . . . just leave it somewhere," Minou spluttered.

"Don't make things difficult," her sister said irritably.

"But I have to at least say goodbye, surely?"

"Say goodbye? Who to? Your human? Are you crazy? He might not let you go. He'll lock you up."

"Let me at least say goodbye to the Tatter Cat," Minou cried unhappily. "And explain what's happening . . . It's only four roofs away."

"You stay here," her sister hissed. "*I'll* take care of it . . . otherwise you'll just let him talk you into staying. Wait for me here. I'll see the Tatter Cat there in your gutter."

And off she went, over the dimly lit rooftops, passing Bibi's attic window on her way to Tibble's gutter.

When she came back she said, "I have to wish you luck."

"Who from?" Minou asked quickly.

"Not your human," her sister said. "I did see him. He came to the window and I left in a hurry. But the Tatter Cat wishes you luck. She said she hopes you'll drop by soon when you have a tail again. She said I look just like you!"

* * *

Now it was morning and sunny.

For hours, Minou had been sitting in a toolshed in the back garden of the house on Victoria Avenue. Next to the lawnmower. She was still shivering a little, more from excitement than from the cold. But soon I'll have fur, she thought. Soon . . . with any luck.

They hadn't had any luck yet. Her sister hadn't been able to catch a dusk thrush.

"Is it going to take much longer?" Minou asked through the half-open door of the tool shed. "The sun's already up."

"Yes, great, just *hurry* me, will you?" her sister snapped. "It's a tremendous help, you hurrying me. . . . But I'll go and check the front garden."

From the toolshed Minou could see the back of the house where she had been born and where she had lived as a young cat.

Soon she'd be allowed to go back inside and get a saucer of milk and be patted. And when she started purring, no one would say, "Shame on you, Miss Minou!"

Here in the garden, she knew every tree and every shrub. In the old days she had caught frogs here on the lawn and once she had even caught a mole. She had scratched in the flower beds. Digging a little hole between the begonias and then sitting over it with a quivering tail and thoughtful eyes, the way cats do.

And then scratching the soil to cover it up again when she was finished. She was starting to feel more and more cattish.

It was going to work, she could feel it in her bones. Very soon now . . .

Then she was shocked by a terrible cheeping sound.

Her ginger sister was running toward her. She had nabbed one of the dusk thrushes from the front garden. In that same instant, Tibble and Bibi were standing at the front hedge, but Minou didn't know that. Her sister trotted up triumphantly.

She couldn't say anything with her mouth full of thrush, but in her eyes you could see her thinking, Who's the best hunter around?

The bird chirped and cheeped and fluttered hopelessly between her sister's cruel jaws. For a second, Minou thought, Mmmm, yummy!

But when her ginger sister came closer, Minou hit her hard and yelled, "Let go!"

Her sister jumped and released her prey. The dusk thrush immediately flew off, wobbling and unsteady at first . . . then straight up into the sky, twittering its way to freedom.

"*That* is the last straw," her sister said in a quiet voice full of menace.

"I . . . I'm sorry . . . ," Minou said. She was utterly ashamed of herself.

"*This* really is the end," her sister hissed angrily. "I've been running around all night for you . . . all night. Finally, using all my strength and all my cunning, I catch a rare dusk thrush for you. Because I know that it's your last chance . . . because you're my sister. And *look what you've done!*"

"I couldn't help it," Minou spluttered. "I didn't stop to think."

"You didn't stop to think! That's a fine remark. After

140

everything I've done for you . . . You knock the bird out of my mouth. *Bah!*"

"I'd done it before I even realized," Minou moaned. "And there is *another* one—didn't you say there were two of them?"

"You don't think I'm going to go hunting for you again, do you?" Her sister was now beside herself with rage.

"You know what you are? You're a *human*! You're just like that Woman of mine. That Woman of *ours*, because she used to be yours too. She eats *chicken*, but if we catch a bird it's, *Oh, no!* Then she knocks the birds right out of our mouths. Remember? When you lived here . . . Remember? We used to talk about it often. It made you furious. 'The hypocrite,' you said. 'Eating chicken herself and taking our birds off us.'"

"I remember," Minou said.

"So why did you just do exactly the same thing?"

"I don't know. I think I've changed."

"You've changed *too much*," her sister said. "You'll never recover. And now it's over. You're not my sister anymore. Go away. Get out of my garden for good. And watch out if I ever see you here again!"

She hissed so viciously that Minou fled . . . farther into the back garden. And then through a hole in the hedge into the next garden and farther, through garden after garden, with her sister's hissing screech still audible far behind her.

As she wandered on, she thought about what had happened.

How could something like that even be possible? All the while she had longed to hunt and catch birds again. Why had she done something so unnatural? So *uncattish*?

Saving a bird . . . what an idiotic thing to do.

As she walked she tried to work it out. I could *imagine* the bird's pain, she thought. I could *imagine* how frightened it was. But if you can imagine something like that, you're not a cat anymore. Not at all. Cats never feel sorry for birds. *Ever*. I think I've let my last chance slip by.

—19—
CARLO THIS TIME

The weather changed while Tibble and Bibi were still on their way back to their own neighborhood. The wind got up, big clouds drifted over, and raindrops started to fall.

"Will you be on time for school?" Tibble asked.

"Easy," said Bibi. "It's nowhere near half eight yet."

They had reached Green Square and Tibble said, "Let's shelter from the rain for a bit. That bench under the trees is dry." They sat down and sucked their peppermints, feeling a little sad.

I've got my job back, thought Tibble. And I don't have to move out of my flat anymore. So everything's worked out. I've just lost my secretary. And I don't have a Cat Press Agency. No more news from cats. I'll have to do it myself. Am I up to it? Am I brave enough?

"Of course I am," he told himself sternly. "I'm not even that shy anymore. I'm brave enough to go up to all kinds of people to ask them questions. And having to do it myself will actually be good for me. But I'm still not happy. You'd think I'd be a tiny bit happy, but I'm not."

Miss Minou . . . he thought. There were so many things I wanted to ask her. Before she changed back to a cat. And did I ever actually thank her? No, never. I always told her off for acting too cattish. And I never even paid her either. Not that money would be any use to her now.

That thought didn't make him any happier. Just a pair of gloves . . . that's all I ever gave her . . . and that was only because I was scared she'd scratch someone. If she ever comes back—as a person, even if she's a very cattish kind of person—I'll never get angry again. She can hiss sometimes if she likes. And purr too. And rub up against people. She was actually sweetest of all when she was purring. *Purrfect*, thought Tibble. And then a dog barked just behind their bench.

It was a Great Dane. It was standing under a tree and barking at something in the branches.

Without a word, Tibble and Bibi jumped up and went over to look. The dog was making an enormous racket and leapt up against the trunk like a wild thing until its master called it. "Carlo!" he called. "Here, boy. Sit!"

Carlo whimpered for a moment, then obeyed.

Tibble and Bibi stood there looking up in the rain that was dripping down from the leaves, and there, very high up in the branches, they saw a leg and a shoe. The milk van came round the corner to Green Square.

"Excuse me, could you help for a moment?" Tibble asked. "My secretary is up a tree. And she's too scared to come down."

"It was a dog, I suppose," the milkman said. "It happens all the time. We're used to it round here. Hang on, I'll park the van under the tree."

Two minutes later Minou was down at street level again and the milkman had driven off. She was wet and her clothes were covered with green smudges, but that didn't matter. Tibble and Bibi were both grinning with relief, and they both wrapped an arm around her wet shoulders.

"How wonderful," Tibble said. "It's fantastic! It was all just our imagination! It wasn't true at all! We just let ourselves get carried away!"

"What wasn't true?" Minou asked.

The rain had grown heavier and they were getting wetter and wetter, but none of them felt it.

"We saw you early this morning, Miss Minou," Tibble said. "At least, we thought it was you."

"A ginger cat," Bibi said. "First on the rooftops!"

"That was my sister," said Minou. "My quintuplet sister. We're very similar."

"And then in Victoria Avenue," Tibble said. "We went there and we saw that cat again. With a thrush."

"Yes, that was her too. My sister."

"But we're all getting drenched! Let's go home!" Tibble cried.

And when he said that—"Let's go home!"—he felt so enormously happy that he wanted to burst into song right there in the middle of the street.

"I can't come with you," Bibi said sadly. "I have to go to

school. And now I won't hear about everything that's happened."

"Come to our place as soon as school's finished," Minou said. "Then I'll tell the whole story all over again."

Sopping wet, Tibble and Minou arrived at the attic, where all the cats were waiting for them. Fluff and the Tatter Cat and the little kittens all crowded around their feet, meowing and purring.

"We'll put on some dry clothes first," Tibble said. "Then you can tell me everything."

Minou told him what had happened. About her sister. And about why she'd left without saying anything first.

"After all, I'd always been so desperate to turn back into a cat," she said. "At least, I thought so. And when it finally came down to it, I didn't want to anymore. I spent an awfully long time shilly-shallying."

"And that's over now?" Tibble asked.

"I think so," said Minou. "My shilly-shallying is over. I want to be a human. But I'm afraid a lot of my cattish traits are here to stay. I just shot up that tree, for instance. When the dog came."

"That's fine," said Tibble.

"And I can feel that I'm going to start purring again."

"It's all fine," said Tibble. "Purr away. And you can hiss and rub up against people too."

"Hissing's not necessary at the moment," said Minou. "But a nice little head rub . . ."

"Be my guest," said Tibble.

Minou rubbed her head against his shoulder. It was a very wet head, because her red hair was still far from dry.

"I . . . I was s-so scared," Tibble stuttered. "So scared I'd never see you again, Miss Minou. It's only just sinking in how terrible I felt when you were gone. Don't run away again like that. Please! Promise me that!"

"I won't run away again," Minou said. "But I was worried you didn't need me anymore. Now that you've got over your shyness."

"I need you so much, Minou," Tibble said. "Not just as a secretary, but also . . ." He blushed. "Well . . . I just need you," he said. "Here in the house, with me. Do you understand what I'm saying, Minou?"

He noticed that he'd grabbed hold of her hand. And that he'd stopped calling her *Miss* Minou. He let go again and looked away nervously. Until now she'd always insisted on that *Miss*. And she'd always called him *Mr.* Tibble. But now she just smiled and said, "I'd love some breakfast, Tibble. A whole tin of sardines. And after that I'll just pop out onto the roof for a second. The Tatter Cat says she'd like to talk to me in private for a moment."

"Do that first, then," said Tibble. "And in the meantime I'll get a big breakfast ready with all kinds of yummy things." He set to work in the kitchen, and Minou and the Tatter Cat went out through the window and onto the roof.

"Something's wrong," said Minou. "What is it? You look like you're not glad to see me back."

"Of course I'm glad you're back," said the Tatter Cat. "That's not it at all. It's just . . . Look, I don't respect you anymore. . . . What can I say? This latest thing is just too much."

"What? Coming back here?"

"No, I'm talking about this business with that thrush and your sister! I've seen plenty in all my years as a stray, but nothing like this. Feeling pity for a thrush! It makes me want to puke! Next thing you'll pity a fish. You'll go up to the fishmonger and knock the fish right out of his paws . . . sorry . . . his hands. Never mind me, I'm a bit upset."

"Yes, you could tone things down a little," said Minou.

"And I wanted to tell you that I'm heading off again too," said the Tatter Cat. "I'm going back to being a stray. My kids are already eating from saucers. As far as I'm concerned, you can start giving them away. They don't need me anymore. Oh yeah, I've got some news for you too. Just heard it from the Deodorant Cat. The perfume factory expansion is off. The councillor refused to approve it. Tell your human."

"Thanks," said Minou.

"Because the Cat Press Agency will be continuing as normal, won't it?" the Tatter Cat asked.

"Sure, everything will continue as normal."

"And you'll be back in your box?" the Tatter Cat asked. "To sleep?"

"Of course," said Minou. "Why not?"

"Oh . . . I don't know." The Tatter Cat stared at her mistrustfully with her yellow eyes. She was looking very battered and grimy again. "You know," she said softly, "I suddenly had a feeling you were going to marry him."

"What gives you *that* idea?" Minou asked.

"It was just a feeling . . . ," the Tatter Cat said. "And I'm just warning you. If you do that, you'll have blown it completely. You'll never be able to turn back into a cat. And maybe it'll get so bad that you won't be able to talk to us anymore. You won't understand Cattish. You'll even forget the Yawl-Yowl Song."

"We'll cross that bridge when we get to it," said Minou.

Tibble leant out of the kitchen window and called, "Breakfast is ready! For cats and people!"

"Come on," said Minou. "Let's go inside."

ANNIE M. G. SCHMIDT (1911–1995) was regarded as the Queen of Dutch Children's Literature, and her books have been an essential part of every Dutch childhood for the last fifty years. She trained as a librarian but burst onto the literary scene when the newspaper she was working for discovered her gift for children's verse. Having won numerous awards during her lifetime, including the Hans Christian Andersen Award, Schmidt is now included in the canon of Dutch history taught to all Dutch schoolchildren, alongside Spinoza, Anne Frank, and Vincent van Gogh.

DAVID COLMER has won several international awards for his translations of Dutch and Flemish novels, poetry, and children's books. He has translated much of Annie M. G. Schmidt's work.

YEARLING

Turning children into readers for more than fifty years.

**Classic and award-winning literature for every shelf.
How many have you checked out?**

**Find the perfect book, play games,
and meet favorite authors at RandomHouseKids.com!**